WITF

MW00699353

A ℬODKIN
for the
ℬRIDE

Wisteria Tearoom Mysteries

A BODKIN for the BRIDE

PATRICE GREENWOOD

Book View Café
Cedar Crest, New Mexico

AUG '17

This is a work of fiction. All of the characters, organizations, and events portrayed in this novel are either products of the author's imagination or are used fictitiously.

A BODKIN FOR THE BRIDE

An Evennight Book
Published by Book View Café Publishing Cooperative
P.O. Box 1624
Cedar Crest, NM 87008

www.bookviewcafe.com

Cover photo: Chris Krohn

ISBN: 978-1-61138-496-3

First Edition July 2015

Printed in the United States of America

in loving memory of
Darragh Edmund Nagle

Acknowledgments

My thanks to my wonderful publication team for their help with this novel: Sherwood Smith, Phyllis Irene Radford, Pari Noskin, and Chris Krohn; to my faithful consultants Ken and Marilyn Dusenberry; and to my colleagues in Book View Café.

Thanks also to Mary Alice Higbie and the staff of the St. James Tearoom, for inspiring me to write this series, for making Wisteria White tea a reality, and for continuing to make me welcome.

For who would bear the whips and scorns of time,
Th' oppressor's wrong, the proud man's contumely,
The pangs of despised love, the law's delay,
The insolence of office, and the spurns
That patient merit of th' unworthy takes,
When he himself might his quietus make
With a bare bodkin?

—William Shakespeare, *Hamlet*

1

"YOU SURE YOU'LL FIND THEM HERE?" I asked as I walked with my aunt toward the entrance of the Tesuque Pueblo Flea Market.

"Yes, I was here last week, and I saw the perfect buttons," said Nat, putting on sunglasses and hefting her woven shoulder bag. "I don't know why I didn't just buy them then."

"Because you didn't have the fabric yet?"

"Maybe."

The sun pounded down from a blinding turquoise sky, already hot though it wasn't yet nine o'clock, making me glad I'd brought my garden hat. Late September was still warm in Santa Fe. We'd always called it Indian Summer, though perhaps that was no longer an acceptable term. Still, the Indians I knew continued to refer to themselves as Indians. I had long since decided not to worry about it.

We trudged uphill through the dusty parking lot to the market's painted plywood entrance. Beyond the flea market, at the very top of the hill, the complicated roof of the Santa Fe Opera house peeped above the piñon trees. I paused to gaze at it, feeling a pang as I remembered the murders that had occurred there during the summer. Losing Vi Benning had broken the hearts of everyone at my tearoom, mine included. I swallowed, sending her silent well-wishes, wherever she was.

"Ellen!"

Nat beckoned to me from the market's entrance, and I hurried to catch up with her. We passed through, declined the offer of a free Tesuque Pueblo Flea Market bumper sticker, and joined the strolling crowd admiring fine art, oriental rugs, imports from Mexico and Guatemala, clothing, baskets, and pottery. This was not your average flea market. Some of the booths were permanent structures complete with floors, practically usable as living space, though made of plywood. Others were tables beneath shade awnings more like what the words "flea market" would normally conjure. Some fell between these extremes: enclosed tents or booths with walls, even an old-style chrome trailer-camper with the owner's goods spread out beneath its shade canopy. There was not much rhyme or reason to the layout.

The market catered to the tourist crowd, but with enough good prices that the locals frequented it as well. Nat led me toward the back, where a long, tent-shaded area was reserved for whatever artisans from the Pueblo were inclined to set up. Today there were half a dozen: two jewelers, a table of knives with inlaid stone handles, a woman selling sage smudge sticks and handmade dolls of Indian women, a baker with fresh *horno* bread, and a potter.

"Oh, good, he's here," Nat murmured, and stepped up to one of the jeweler's tables to inspect a basket full of silver buttons. I strolled on toward the baker's table.

The bread was wrapped in clear plastic bags, all the loaves basically round but with different shapes made by manipulating the dough before letting it rise. Iz Naranjo, one of my servers at the Wisteria Tearoom, who came from Tesuque Pueblo, had told me how each family group had its own traditional patterns. The bread was baked communally in the beehive-shaped outdoor ovens, called *hornos*, that could be seen at every pueblo in New Mexico, and the shapes were how different families identified their loaves. Even villages that had gone to more modern housing still had *hornos* behind many of the homes.

I picked up a loaf with four chubby points poking out of its roundness. It still felt slightly warm through the plastic; baked that morning, then. I wondered if Julio would be interested in making shaped breads—smaller versions—for the tearoom.

A skinny guy in jeans and a plaid shirt over a t-shirt stepped up beside me and spoke in a low voice to the booth's owner, a tall, heavy-set Pueblo man. The owner took out a loaf from beneath the table—this one decorated with some kind of knot made from two strips of dough, almost making the loaf look gift-wrapped—and handed it to his customer, then palmed the bill he was given in exchange.

"That's a pretty design," I said as the younger man left. "How much?"

"That was the last one," said the owner with a smile. "Sorry. That one's five dollars." He gestured to the loaf in my hands.

"Thanks," I said, and set it down. I didn't need an entire loaf of bread calling to me from the kitchen over the weekend. I could buy it for Nat and Manny, but they probably didn't need to carbo-load either.

I knew that some families kept special bread designs just for themselves. To show that I wasn't offended by being denied the knot-decorated loaf, I paid two dollars for a small plastic bag holding half a dozen *biscochitos*. I tucked the cookies into my purse and ambled to the next booth, with the smudge sticks and dolls.

The latter were in jewel-toned traditional dresses, their black yarn hair done in classic squash-blossom style, gathered into two rounded buns standing slightly away from either side of the head. A doll in a red velvet dress, very like the dress Nat and I were making for her wedding, made me smile and I picked it up.

Both the Pueblo people and the Navajo wore such dresses: actually skirt-and-blouse sets, the long-sleeved, cuffed blouse worn over the skirt and usually belted with a concho belt. I was making one of these dresses for myself, too, since I was Nat's maid of honor. Mine would be blue.

"Twenty dollars," said the woman behind the table, her squared black glasses at odds with her moon-shaped face. I nodded; it was a good price for a handmade doll. The detail was lovely, down to the small concho belt and squash-blossom necklace, though of course these weren't made of silver.

I considered getting the doll as a gift for Nat, but decided against it for now. I could always change my mind later. The wedding was a few weeks away, still.

"Thank you," I said, setting the doll down and moving on to the next table.

The proprietor, a young man in a crisp denim shirt and jeans, gave me a shy glance and an almost-smile. I smiled back.

The knives were beautiful, with inlaid strips and triangles of multicolored stone on the hilts. Turquoise, purple sugilite, coral, lapis, and others I couldn't name made the handles into works of art, but I felt reluctant to touch them. I still had uncomfortable feelings about knives since the murders at the Opera over the summer and wasn't inclined to buy one, however lovely. If the artist could make a belt-buckle in a similar style, it might make a nice gift for Manny. I glanced up to ask him, but he was staring toward the baker's table.

"Ellen, come and look at these," Nat called.

I joined her at the jeweler's table. She showed me two different, round, silver buttons with stamped designs. One had a classic triple-cloud design with falling rain, the other bore a flower.

"Which do you like?"

"The storm clouds might not be the best omen for a harmonious marriage," I said.

"But it's rain!" Nat said. "Prosperity! Besides, Manny and I don't argue."

"Much."

"You like the flower better, then?"

I took the second button in my hand. "It is pretty simple. Sweet-looking, though."

"I think I'll go with the rain."

I secretly agreed with her, and when she suggested I get the flowers for my dress, I insisted on getting the rain clouds to match hers. In New Mexico, rain is almost always considered a blessing.

Nat wouldn't let me help with the cost of the buttons. "No, no; I'm buying all the materials. It's the least I can do, since you're helping me make the dresses."

"I like sewing," I said as we walked away from the tent.

"Good, because I'm barely competent to assist. I can sew these buttons on, but forget about making buttonholes."

I chuckled. "I'll do the buttonholes. It'll be fun. I haven't made anything but curtains since I bought the house."

The house that had become the Wisteria Tearoom. My sanctuary, my home, my future. Prosperity would be the key to its success, and consequently my own. I thought of the rain-cloud buttons with satisfaction.

"Did you want to look at anything else?" Nat asked.

I shook my head. "Let's start sewing. It would be nice to get at least one dress finished today."

We plodded through the dusty parking lot back to Nat's car, and were at her house in less than five minutes. I breathed a sigh of relief as we entered the shady coolness of the old adobe building. Nat had bought it with her first husband, Uncle Stephen, gone these seven years. I wondered if Manny would move in after the wedding.

Nat hadn't mentioned their plans. I couldn't imagine her leaving the house, though. So many memories. So many good times.

"Limeade?" she offered.

"Yes, please."

I went into the living room, where Nat had set up one of the long tables she used for the occasional big barbecue parties she and Manny threw. Bags of fabric and notions sat on it, along with the patterns.

My portable sewing machine sat on a smaller card table nearby. I unpacked it and set it up, plugging it into a surge-protected power strip I'd brought along as insurance against the sometimes-unreliable ancient wiring of Nat's house. Then I fished a spool of dark red thread out of the fabric store bags and sat down to wind a bobbin.

"I sent out the invitations," Nat said, setting an icy glass beside me. "You should get yours in a day or two."

I took a sip, enjoying the cold, sweet, puckery lime. "Thanks."

"You going to bring your boyfriend to the wedding?"

"He's not my boyfriend."

Nat raised an eyebrow and I could feel myself blushing. She had been there the day Tony kissed me in front of the whole tearoom staff.

But he wasn't my boyfriend. We had been on one actual date (other than the Opera, which had been a party), and that had ended in an argument. A couple of other times we'd gone out for a drink or a quick, impromptu meal. Those didn't count.

I finished winding the bobbin and started threading the machine. I liked Tony Aragón. He was undeniably attractive, but he was also a cop and that made things a bit difficult. His world was very different from mine.

I knew that I would eventually have to make a choice. Remembering that kiss, I swallowed. There was no way to pretend that it hadn't happened, that the potential for more wasn't there. I felt that potential, and I knew Tony felt it too, and it wouldn't be fair to string him along. I'd have to decide, and pretty soon, whether I wanted an intimate relationship with him.

Not today, I told myself. I had other things to deal with today.

The machine was ready. Time to commit. I got up and took the red velvet out of its bag, setting aside the blue. Ran my hands over the lush pile, then folded the fabric with the right sides together and spread it on the table for cutting.

Nat had already separated the pattern pieces and ironed them. She could sew, but she had deferred to me on this project. I laid the pieces for the skirt onto the velvet and tacked them with a few pins, adding my sewing weights to make sure nothing shifted. When I was satisfied I took up my shears and looked at Nat, who was observing from an armchair, sipping limeade.

"Ready?"

She nodded.

The bite of the shears through the velvet evoked a little thrill that I remembered from my first sewing project. There was no going back from here. I was changing that lush fabric, molding it into a new shape.

Nat offered to gather the tiers of the skirt while I pieced together the blouse and started sewing the seams. As the dress began to take shape, I pictured Nat wearing it, standing in my garden, surrounded by friends and family and Manny, her husband-to-be. Would Tony be a part of this picture? I wasn't sure.

He was bringing his mother and grandmother to tea at last, on Saturday. It had only taken three or four reminders to get him to book a reservation; I'd begun to wonder if he really didn't want to bring his family into my den of Anglophilic Victoriana.

But he'd finally set a date. I had given him a gift card that would cover tea for all of them, and Tony had asked me to join them.

Meeting the family. A step forward. Maybe after spending some time with them all, I would know whether it was a good idea to invite Tony to the wedding.

Nat and I worked on the dress until we got hungry, Nat pinning and me sewing, then we stopped for chicken salad and gazpacho. Whatever confidence Nat lacked in the sewing department, she more than made up for in the kitchen. The gazpacho was crisp and cold, with just the right amount of texture.

"What's Manny up to today?" I asked.

"Looking for a mariachi band."

"Mariachis? I thought you wanted the wedding to be quiet..."

"I do. Don't worry, dear, we won't blast out your neighbors with loud music. I told him an acoustic trio at most."

"I'm not worried about the neighbors."

Though the tearoom was in a Victorian house, the neighborhood had become a commercial area. Originally part of the Fort Marcy military park, it was close to Santa Fe's plaza, and all those old houses had long since been occupied by businesses. I happened to live upstairs from mine, but I was an exception to the rule.

The wedding would be in my garden, and the reception

indoors in the tearoom. The original plan was for only a few friends, but of course the guest list had grown. Like many Hispanic families, Manny's was extensive, and he wanted to share his good fortune with a lot of them. I didn't mind, but I was beginning to worry that the party would outgrow the tearoom's capacity.

Nat was philosophical about it. This was her second wedding. Her closest friends and family were invited, and she seemed happy to let Manny add as many of his friends and family as he wished.

I finished the waistband on Nat's skirt and stood up to shake it out. Turning it right side out, I admired the sheen of the velvet, now rippling in richly-gathered tiers. Nat stood and I held the skirt up to her waist.

"Oh, Ellen! It's gorgeous!"

"Well, it's not done. The waistband needs elastic."

"I'll do that. Where's your threader-thing?"

I handed her the skirt and dug in my sewing box, retrieving a slender metal implement that looked like an overgrown pair of tweezers. "It's called a bodkin."

"Funny word."

"It's an old word. Shakespeare used it."

"Shakespeare used this?" She held up the bodkin.

"No, silly. He used the *word*. It also means a dagger."

"You're so good at history," she said, poking through the fabric bags. "I can never remember things like that."

Nat found a package of elastic and sat down with the bodkin and the skirt, while I went back to work on the tunic. We kept at it until the afternoon light began to slant through the windows to the west.

I finished a seam and stood up to stretch, then sighed. "I don't think we're going to get it all done today."

"Stay for dinner."

"No, I promised to get together with Gina. Movie night." I started tidying, putting my things in my basket and shutting off the sewing machine.

"Tomorrow?" Nat said, gathering scraps of velvet from the table. "Or are you working?"

Mondays were theoretically my second weekend days, but more often than not I spent them getting ready for the week at the tearoom. Julio, my chef, came in for half a day most weeks.

"I might get some time in the afternoon. I'll call you."

"All right, dearest. Thank you so much."

I gave Nat a hug. "Thanks for lunch. Smooch Manny for me."

"I'll tell him it's from you."

Smile lines crinkled the corners of her eyes, and for an instant I saw an echo of my father's face in hers. Biting down on the pang of grief, I smiled back.

"Talk to you soon."

I was digging my keys out of my purse as I stepped out the front door, so I was at my car door before I saw the body.

2

I FROZE. Halfway down the driveway, masked in the lengthening shadows of early evening, a man lay face down on the gravel slope. Fear of doing the wrong thing kept me immobile for a few seconds. I'd found a body before, and it was stressful beyond belief.

The thought that he might still be alive jolted me into action. I hurried down the slope, my loafers slipping a little on the deep gravel as I pulled my cell phone out of my purse. I punched 911 and then gingerly knelt beside the man.

Homeless, was my first instinct. His clothes—jeans and a denim shirt—were dirty and torn in a couple of places, and his black hair was a mess.

I gritted my teeth, took a deep breath, and touched his wrist. It wasn't warm.

"Police dispatch," said a female voice on my phone. "What is your emergency?"

"I just found a man in the driveway," I said, feeling short of breath. "I think he may be dead."

"What address?"

I gave it to her. Glanced toward the house, wondering if I should get Nat. The sky was patched with clouds, not enough for rain but enough to cast a chill over the early evening.

"Is he breathing?"

I looked back at the man. "I don't know...he's face down."

"Can you turn him over?"

A flash of memory—Tony scowling at me—*You realize that's tampering with evidence.* But he'd admitted later that I'd done right to try to see if Sylvia could be saved.

I swallowed. "I'll try. Hold on."

I put the phone down and gingerly pushed at the guy's uphill side. He budged, so I steeled myself to push harder until I succeeded in rolling him onto his back.

"Oh!"

I choked back a sob. His face was bruised and swollen. He looked Indian. Probably from Tesuque, it was the nearest pueblo.

My phone made a noise. I picked it up.

"I'm here. He's been beaten."

"I'm sending an ambulance. Can you tell if he has a pulse?"

"Hang on."

I tried feeling his wrist, then his throat, but I was scared and didn't know how to find a pulse. His skin was cold. Holding my breath, I put my ear to his chest. I heard nothing.

I straightened up, aware that my own pulse was rocketing. "I'm pretty sure there's no pulse," I told the dispatcher, my voice quavering. "Not breathing."

A siren began to wail in the distance.

He was dead. In that moment, I was sure.

The dispatcher kept me talking. I answered her questions, feeling numb as I looked down at the stranger's poor, abused face. Not homeless, I decided. His skin didn't have that leathery texture that people get from poor nutrition and living outdoors. He seemed fairly young, from what I could tell.

The sun was setting and the temperature was dropping. The sirens got louder. I thought of warning Nat, but decided I should stay where I was.

The wailing became painful, then stopped abruptly. A squad car turned into the driveway and skidded to a stop with a crunch of gravel. It backed out and moved a short way up the street.

Seconds later a rescue squad pulled up and two men jumped out. One of them ran toward me while the other went to the back of the vehicle.

"They're here," I said into my phone.

"All right, ma'am. Give them the details."

"Thanks. Bye."

The EMT—blond, muscular, probably a former quarterback —dropped to his knees on the other side of the dead man and put a hand to his throat, then looked up at me, frowning.

"How long has he been here?"

"I don't know. I called the minute I found him."

The other tech came up, carrying a box of medical stuff. He was shorter and darker, stocky. "'Scuse me," he said without making eye contact.

I got out of his way, standing and taking a couple of steps back. The two techs traded a glance and the first one shook his head.

A car door chunked shut and I saw a uniformed policewoman jogging toward me. A door slam from the direction of the house made me turn. Nat had come out and stood on the *portal*, staring down toward the mess.

"Ellen Rosings?" said the cop as she reached me.

I glanced at her. "Yes—my aunt—it's her house."

I started toward Nat and the cop came along. "Don't go down there, Nat," I said. "There's nothing you can do."

"Ms. Rosings, I need ask you a few questions." The cop looked at Nat. "Is there somewhere we could talk?"

Nat was frowning down the driveway, but at this question she looked at the cop. "Yes. Come in. I'd better make some coffee. What happened?"

"I don't know," I said. "I just found him when I was about to leave."

"Where could we talk?" asked the cop.

I looked at her, noting her impatience. Maybe she didn't want me to discuss things with Nat before answering her questions. She was Hispanic, hair pulled back in an efficient bun. A little shorter than I, and wiry. Not as bulky as the body armor made her look.

"We could go in the living room," I said. "OK, Nat?"

My aunt nodded, worry making tight lines around her mouth. "I'll bring the coffee in."

I led the cop through the kitchen and dining room, past the work table that we had left up—piled with fabric and Nat's half-finished dress—to a couple of chairs by the empty kiva fireplace.

Late sunlight slanted in from the western windows; I closed the blinds, then took a seat.

The cop took out a tablet. "I'll need your name, phone number, address."

I gave them to her, then answered her questions, most of which the dispatcher had also asked me. The initial stress of finding the body had faded, leaving me feeling sad and tired.

"Is the man outside someone you know, or someone you've seen in the neighborhood?"

I shook my head.

"Has there been any trouble in your aunt's family?"

"No. I don't think he has anything to do with us. He might have been looking for help, but..." I shrugged.

The house wasn't far from the frontage road of the highway that ran north from Santa Fe. If someone had trouble on that road and went seeking help on foot, Nat's could easily be the first driveway they came to.

"Have you had any contact from strangers recently? Wrong numbers or hang-ups?"

"I don't live here. You should ask my aunt."

"I will, but I'm asking you, too. That's your car outside, right?"

"Yes. You're thinking he followed me here?"

"It's possible."

She met my gaze, waiting. I didn't like the feeling I got from her—a low-key, underlying hostility—but Tony had been like that, too, at first.

"No, I haven't had any strange calls lately, or anything like that," I said.

She made a note on her tablet, then looked up as Nat came in with a tray holding a half-full pot of coffee and two cups. She put it down on the low table before me and straightened.

"I'm going to take some coffee down to the paramedics," she said. "I'll be back in a couple minutes."

The cop made no objection as Nat left. I picked up the pot. "Would you like some?"

"Sure. Thanks."

I poured, then added sugar and cream to my cup and took a big swallow. I suspected it would be a long evening.

Gina! Movie night!

I reached in my purse for my phone. "Excuse me, do you mind if I make a call? I was supposed to be somewhere tonight."

"Go ahead."

The cop kept making notes on her tablet, and didn't offer me privacy. I punched Gina's number and stood, pacing a few steps away.

Gina picked up, and I could hear the grin in her voice. "If you're calling to offer to bring wine, don't bother. I've got lots."

"Gina, I'm not going to make it. I'm still at Nat's. There's— well, there's a sort of emergency."

"Is Nat all right?" Her voice had gone serious.

"She's fine. It's just—um, I found a guy in her driveway. The police are here."

"Oh, crap. Was this guy dead?"

"Yeah."

"Ellen, you have to stop finding bodies."

"This is only the second one!"

In a year.

"Third," she said. "You found Vi."

"Not by myself! There was a whole group of us." I glanced toward the cop, who was, of course, listening. "Look, I'd better go. I'll call you later. Sorry about dinner."

"I'll save some for you. Come by when you're free."

"You don't have to do that."

"Hey, you've gotta eat, and I made a whole pan of lasagna. I'm not going to eat it all myself. I'll just do my nails in the meantime."

"I'll call you."

"OK. Take care, hon."

"Thanks."

I returned to my chair and put the phone away. Took another swig of coffee. The cop hadn't touched hers.

"So you'd never seen this guy before?"she asked.

I bit back impatience at the question I'd already answered twice. "No. At first I thought he was homeless."

"Why?"

"Because his clothes were dirty and torn. I didn't realize until I turned him over that he must have been in a fight."

"So he was face down when you found him?"

"That's right. I thought I'd said so."

She referred to her tablet. "Yeah, you did. So why do you think he came up here?"

"I have no idea. Like I said, maybe he was looking for help."

I heard the front door close, then Nat's swift footsteps. "Ellen? The policemen outside want to talk to you."

I looked at the cop. She nodded, and stood.

"Ms. Rosings?" she said to Nat.

"No, dear. My name is Wheeler."

"Wheeler, sorry. Can I ask you a few questions?"

I headed outside, relieved to be off the witness chair. The sun had almost set by now, and several more emergency vehicles had arrived: two squad cars; a third, unmarked, black sports car that had a spotlight and multiple antennae; and an ambulance. As I walked down the drive the ambulance pulled away, and I realized the body was gone.

"Here she is," said the quarterback EMT, who was standing with two uniformed cops and a guy in jeans and a western shirt. They all turned to look at me.

"Miss Rosings?" said the plainclothes guy. He was tall, with a craggy face, brown hair and mustache, and sharp eyes. He pulled out a badge case and flipped it open just long enough for me to see a glimpse of gold inside. "I'm Zeke Walters. I've been assigned to your case."

It isn't my case.

I kept the thought to myself and swallowed disappointment that Tony wasn't here instead. I gave him a civil nod. "Hello."

He asked me a couple of the same questions I'd been asked twice before. I tried to answer patiently.

"Ever seen the guy before?" Walter said.

"No."

"You sure?"

"I didn't recognize him," I said. "At first I thought he was homeless."

"Too clean." He reached toward one of the cops, who handed him a plastic evidence bag. He showed it to me. "This yours?"

The bag held a knife, which sent my memory spinning back a few weeks to when Tony and I had found the knife used to murder Victor Solano. My pulse took a jump.

"No," I said, frowning as I saw the colored shapes on the handle, "but it looks familiar. May I look closer?"

He handed me the bag. "Don't open it."

Holding it gingerly, I carried it to a patch of sunlight. Turquoise, malachite, and sugilite glowed mutely inside the plastic.

"It looks like some knives I saw at the flea market this morning."

Walters took the bag back. "The Indian flea market?"

"Yes. My aunt and I went there to buy some buttons."

"Where'd you go after that?"

"We came back here and sewed all day. I was about to leave when I found...that poor man."

The detective's eyes narrowed. I didn't like the way he looked at me, but I'd endured enough interrogation in the past few months that I wasn't easily flustered.

After a long pause, Walters took out a cell phone and started punching at it. I debated whether to ask permission to leave or just go, then he held the phone up to me.

"Seen him before?"

The photo looked like a driver's license shot. Young Indian man, pleasant face, not quite smiling. Very familiar.

"Yes," I said slowly. "I think he's the one who was selling the knives."

"Did you talk to him?"

"No. I was going to ask if he could make a belt buckle, but I got distracted."

Walters stared at me, still holding the phone. "What else?"

I shrugged. "That's all I remember."

"You saw him again."

It wasn't a question. I shook my head. "I don't think so."

"Yeah, you did. Right here."

My heart sank. "That's him?"

"Yes ma'am. That's the dead guy."

3

DISMAY FILLED ME. I couldn't find anything to say.

"His name's Daniel Swazo," said Detective Walters. "Ring a bell?"

I shook my head, swallowing, unable to stop staring at the photo and remembering the poor, bruised and swollen face of the body. I couldn't reconcile the two.

"He's from Tesuque Pueblo. Sure you don't know him?"

"I'm sure," I said through a tight throat. "I never saw him before today."

"Why would he follow you here?"

At that, I met the detective's gaze. "How do you know he did?"

"Simple deduction. You were at the flea market, he saw you there. He shows up dead in your driveway. He must have followed you."

"He had no reason to. And it's been hours since we left the market." I took a breath, reminding myself not to get angry. "The frontage road is right there. He was beaten. Maybe he was dumped on the road, and came up here looking for help."

Detective Walters glanced toward the road. "Big coincidence."

"Life is full of coincidences."

He turned back to me with a sour look. I silently chided myself for making what could be construed as a smart remark.

This man made me uncomfortable. I tried to work up the courage to ask if I could leave, but before I got there Nat broke the tension by coming down the driveway with a tray of steaming coffee mugs. I gave her a grateful look.

"Detective Walters, this is my aunt, Natasha Wheeler. This is her house."

"How do, ma'am," he said, then took a mug and slurped at it. "Thanks. Gonna be a cold night."

"Would you like to come inside?"

The female cop who had interviewed me had followed Nat out, and stood looking at Walters. He glanced at her, then shook his head.

"I'll be up in a bit. You go on back in and stay warm."

"May I leave?" I asked him. "I'm expected at a friend's."

"That your car there?"

"Yes."

"Can't move it. Got evidence techs coming to process the scene."

As in crime scene. That could take hours.

"You could call a taxi," Walters offered, watching me narrowly.

I sighed and looked at Nat. "I'll do that if you want me out of your hair."

"No, dear. You're welcome to stay. Which reminds me, I'd better call Manny and warn him not to pull into the driveway. Not that he'd be able to."

Nat gave the last mug of coffee to the quarterback EMT, then started up the driveway. I followed her back to the house, putting away my keys and taking out my phone to call Gina again.

"Oh, pooh!" Gina said after I explained.

"Yeah."

"Come anyway, when you can."

"No, there's no telling when they'll be done. I may end up spending the night."

"I'll put your lasagna in the freezer."

I shook my head, smiling at her determination. When she got hold of an idea, she was sometimes like a terrier with a bone.

We promised each other an evening sometime soon, then said goodbye. I put my phone away, feeling a familiar depression sinking onto me. I jumped up from Manny's armchair, knowing I had to fight it.

Nat was in the kitchen, making a salad. Warm, savory smells were starting to come from the oven.

"Can I help?"

She gave her head a shake, then looked up at me and abruptly stopped. "Sure. Finish cutting up these veggies, and I'll get the butter out."

I took over chopping salad goodies, silently grateful for something to do. Nat knew me better than just about anyone else. She was the only other member of my family still living in Santa Fe, and I leaned on her more than I probably should. It was she who had suggested that I open a tearoom, which had led me out of the deep depression I'd been in since my father died.

I no longer had much time to be depressed. Too much going on.

Being trapped here kept me away from the zillion things I ought to be doing, as well as from my planned evening with Gina. Based on my unfortunately too abundant recent experience of murder investigations, I estimated that the cops would be at work in the driveway until midnight at least.

I became aware that I was frowning and made a conscious effort to stop. Nat and I could sew some more after supper, I told myself. Maybe we'd finish her dress.

The door opened and Manny came into the kitchen, full of bluster and a bit out of breath, his tanned cheeks glowing. "Cops have a dozen cars parked on the street. I had to go up to the top of the hill!"

Nat gave him a smooch. "You're just in time to set the table."

"Good, I'm starving. It smells fantastic! Hi, *hija*," he added, catching my shoulders in one powerful arm.

"Hey, *Tio*," I replied, putting down my knife to hug him back. "*Tio*-to-be."

"Not long now."

He chuckled, then started getting out dishes. He and Nat had been keeping company long enough that he was perfectly at home in her kitchen.

I smiled as I diced the last of the carrots and tossed them into the salad bowl. The prospect of having Manny as my uncle pleased me to no end. He could not have been more different than Uncle Stephen: bulldog-like physique, merry and mischievous, with bristly black hair liberally sprinkled with salt. Stephen had been ethereal by comparison, yet Nat had loved him deeply.

I helped Nat carry the food out to the table. As I went back for the salad dressing, my phone rang. I took it out, and let out a small gasp of relief when I saw that it was Tony calling.

"You OK?" he asked.

"Yes, but I wish you were here."

"I just heard. Don't worry, Zeke is all right."

"Can you come help him?"

"Sorry—it's his baby. Got my hands full anyway. Gang fight. Two dead."

"Oh, no!"

"I'll call you later."

"Be careful, Tony!"

"I'm always careful."

He hung up, abruptly as usual. I'd begun to suspect that he had something against saying goodbye. Swallowing self-pity, I put my phone away, grabbed the bottle of Nat's homemade vinaigrette, and went to the dining room.

"That your boyfriend?" Manny asked.

"He's not my boyfriend."

"Just an acquaintance checking up on you? That's nice."

I did not dignify that with an answer. Instead, I took my seat, and accepted a bowl of green chile chicken stew from Nat.

"Any luck with the musicians?" Nat asked.

"Nah," Manny said. "They wanted me to rent sound equipment. And they had too many trumpets. Whatever happened to strolling mariachis?"

"Maybe you should talk to La Fonda. Don't they have them sometimes?"

"Did you try the talent agencies?" I asked.

Manny shook his head. "I don't want to pay a commission.

I've got a couple more leads."

"Isn't it the musicians who pay the commission?"

"Yeah, well I don't want them to have to pay it."

"I'm sure you'll find someone," said Nat, smiling.

How kind she was. She didn't particularly want mariachis at her wedding, but she knew it meant something to Manny. I doubted I'd have been as patient in her position.

I thought about offering to talk to Ramon, who was an excellent guitarist when he wasn't working in the tearoom's kitchen, but he wasn't a mariachi and might not know anyone to recommend.

"So, Ellen," Manny said. "Tell me about all that." He nodded his head toward the driveway.

"Not over dinner!" Nat protested.

"There isn't that much to tell," I said. "At first I thought it was a homeless guy, but then I saw that he'd been in a fight."

I thought of Tony's gang fight investigation, and wondered fleetingly if the moon was full.

"Some stranger got in a fight and wandered into the driveway to die?" Manny said.

"I think he must have been looking for help. Maybe he came up from the frontage road. And Nat, the police may ask you if you know him."

"They did."

"Well, I saw him at the flea market this morning, in the Tesuque tent. He was selling knives."

Nat's eyes widened in alarm. "Did he talk to you?"

"No, he ignored me, actually. I wanted to ask him a question but his attention was elsewhere."

She frowned. "I don't like this, Ellen."

"The police are thinking he must have followed us, but it doesn't make sense. There were hours between when we came home and when I found him. He couldn't have been lying in the driveway all that time."

Could he? Wouldn't he have been bloated? Smelly? Wouldn't someone have noticed him? I didn't know that much about dead bodies.

Actually, I knew more than I wanted to about them.

"So, I think we can finish your dress tonight," I said.

We talked about the sewing projects for the rest of the meal. Manny showed polite interest, and applauded Nat's choice of buttons. He insisted on helping her with the dishes, and I left them to it, giving them a chance to talk privately.

I went back to the living room and took out Nat's blouse. We had finished the skirt, and I was putting together the sleeves. I made buttonholes in the long cuffs, savoring the rich feel of the velvet under my fingers, the glow of its color in the cove lighting of Nat's living room. I was grateful for a project that required concentration. I didn't want to think about the body.

By the time Nat joined me I was finishing the second sleeve. She sewed buttons on the first one, then we traded and I started fitting the first sleeve into the tunic. We worked in comfortable silence until the doorbell rang. I went with Nat to answer it, and found Detective Walters outside.

"Miss Rosings? I just need to ask you a couple more questions."

"Come in," Nat said before I could step out. "Would you like some coffee?"

"Don't mind if I do. That's very good coffee you make, ma'am."

Nat fussed with mugs and spoons while I invited the detective to sit at the small table in the kitchen nook. I didn't feel like welcoming him farther into her house.

I waited. The detective stared at me. I stared back.

Nat placed a mug of coffee in front of each of us. That distracted him; he looked up and thanked her, took a sip, then cleared his throat.

"So, Miss Rosings." He took a notepad out of his pocket and scribbled on it. "What did you do at the flea market, and who did you talk to?"

I took a swallow of coffee and kept my fingers wrapped around the warm mug. "My aunt wanted to buy some buttons from a vendor she'd seen last week in the Tesuque crafters' tent, so we went straight there when we arrived. While she was shopping for buttons, I looked at the *horno* bread and talked to the man selling it. I bought some *biscochitos* from him. Then I went to the neighboring booth and admired some handmade dolls. Then the next booth was...the man selling knives. The man I found later in the driveway. I wanted to ask him a question but he got distracted, and then my aunt called me over to the jeweler's booth. We discussed the buttons, she bought some, and we left."

He looked up from his notebook, his eyes sharp beneath bushy brows. "That's a good description."

I smiled, but refrained from commenting that I'd had plenty of practice. He must know by now that I'd been interviewed about multiple murders this year.

That probably didn't look good. I could protest all I wanted that it was coincidence, but if I'd learned anything about cops from my acquaintance with Tony, it was that they were perpetually suspicious.

"So the name Daniel Swazo doesn't mean anything to you."

"You told me that was the dead man's name. Otherwise, no."

"How about Tommy Swazo?"

I shook my head. "Sorry."

"Have you ever been up to Tesuque Pueblo?"

"My parents took me to one of their feast days when I was little, but I haven't been back since then."

"Know anyone from the pueblo?"

"One of my employees. Isabel Naranjo."

He scribbled some more. "Did you see her at the flea market?"

"No."

He dumped a large dollop of cream into his coffee, swallowed about half the mug at once, and set it down. "Well, thank you, Miss Rosings. We may have more questions for you later."

"Are your people still working in the driveway?"

"Hm? Oh, no. It's clear now. You can go home."

"Thank you."

I glanced at the clock on Nat's microwave: 10:45, too late to call Gina. I got up to fetch my purse while the detective said goodbye to Nat. When I heard the door close, I came back to the kitchen and took the small plastic bag of *biscochitos* out of my purse.

"I'd forgotten about these. Want one?"

"Sure," Nat said, bringing her own mug of coffee to the table.

The *biscochitos* were mostly intact: only one had broken. Pretty good for an inherently fragile cookie. I set the open bag between us and fished out a half. Nice, crumbly short cookie with just the right hint of anise, generously dusted with cinnamon sugar that stuck to my fingers and made a mess on Nat's table.

"Well, at least we made progress on the dress," Nat said.

"Almost done," I agreed.

"Sorry about your evening with Gina."

I shrugged. "It's not a big deal. At least I got to hang out with you."

I was feeling a little down, but I didn't want Nat to worry, so I chatted about plans for the wedding while we finished the *biscochitos*. Then hugs and goodnight—no, she wouldn't let me help put away the sewing; I was to go straight home and take a hot bath.

"Yes, ma'am," I said, smooching her on the cheek. "I'll call you tomorrow when I know whether I'll have time to come sew some more."

I shouldered my purse and went out to the car. I couldn't help pausing to look toward the bottom of the driveway.

All the signs of police activity were gone, except for the rather churned appearance of the gravel at the foot of the drive. A streetlight cast a sodium-orange glow over it.

I found myself staring at the spot where I'd found Daniel Swazo. Waiting for him to appear, or to manifest in some other way?

I'd been living in a haunted house too long. Shaking myself, I got in my car and headed home.

Monday mornings were usually lazy for me, but while I was lounging in bed I heard someone open the back door downstairs. A minute later the sound of salsa music informed me that it was Julio, my chef.

He wasn't usually this early on Mondays. The tearoom was closed, and he came in only part of the day, to get a head start on the week's baking, making scones to freeze and bake as they were needed.

Sighing for my lost alone time, I got up and dressed, then went downstairs. If Julio was going to rob me of my solitude, the least he could do was make me breakfast.

The smell of eggs and cheese met me at the foot of the stairs. My stomach growled approval. I paused in the butler's pantry to put on a kettle, then continued into the kitchen, where Julio was dancing by the stove.

"Morning, *jefa*! I made you breakfast."

"So I divined. Thank you."

He grinned and gestured toward the table at the back of the kitchen where my staff took their breaks. He'd set it with a full place setting for one, including a chrysanthemum in a bud vase.

"What's the occasion?"

"No occasion. Have a seat, it's ready. You want coffee?"

"Yes, thanks."

I generally prefer tea, but Julio's coffee was very good. He presented me with my favorite breakfast sandwich: green chile cheese croissant, egg over medium, with a slice of cheddar melting over the egg. I began to suspect I was being buttered up.

"Are you having some?" I asked.

"I already ate."

"Well, sit down and keep me company, then."

He helped himself to coffee and did so. I took my time

savoring a bite of the sandwich, then asked him how his weekend had gone.

"Good. I got some great ideas for the menu for October. Want to hear?"

I nodded. He talked about harvest soup and a variation on rumaki, but I could tell from the humming excitement in his limbs that these were not the main thing on his mind. Finally, as I finished the last bite of sandwich, he cast a sidelong glance at me.

"More coffee?"

"No, thanks. Just tell me your brainstorm."

He bit his lip, then took a piece of paper from his pocket and unfolded it. It was an article torn from a magazine, with a photo of cubes, balls, and other geometric shapes outlined in three dimensions, in bright neon colors.

I read the first couple of lines. "Three-D Printing?"

He pointed to the shapes. "Ignore the colors. That's sugar."

"Nice, but—"

"I could program a printer to make little skulls. Sugar skulls, right? For Halloween. Only little ones that can sweeten your tea!" His eyes were alight with creative excitement.

"It's a great idea, Julio, but don't those printers cost a lot of money?"

"It would be worth it. You could sell the sugar shapes in the gift shop. We could make little holly leaves for Christmas, hearts for Valentine's, even Wisteria flowers for the petit fours."

"I like the buttercream wisteria blossoms."

"Well, there's a lot of other stuff we could do with it. All kinds of garnishes for the sweets."

I sighed. "How much does a food-grade 3-D printer cost?"

"I don't know. They're pretty new still."

"I'll ask Kris to dig up some quotes, but don't get your hopes up. We don't have a lot of extra funds in the budget."

Julio nodded, shoulders slumped a bit. "I figured you'd say that."

"Sorry. Next year might be a better bet."

He shrugged and gave me a crooked smile. "Maybe by then

they'll be able to do chocolate."

I got up to take my plate to the dishwashing station. Julio took it from my hands.

"Thanks. May I borrow this?" I waved the article.

"Sure, boss. Thanks for listening."

Feeling bad about disappointing him, I made a pot of tea and carried it up to my office. There I wrote a note to my office manager asking her to find quotes for culinary-grade 3-D printers, clipped it to Julio's article, and set it on her desk in the neighboring office. Returning to my desk, I sat down to a small stack of messages that I hadn't been able to get to on Friday.

Willow Lane had left two of them. I felt a pang of guilt; Willow, the owner of Spirit Tours of Santa Fe, often sank to the bottom half of my priority list. She made me slightly uncomfortable, though she'd proved herself to be not only a class act but sincerely interested in me.

Well, sincerely interested in the tearoom anyway. I had a feeling she cared a lot more about Captain Dusenberry than about me.

I refilled my teacup and fired up my computer. Captain Dusenberry's murder was another subject I had been neglecting of late. Over the summer I'd formed a determination to figure out who had murdered him downstairs in the dining parlor (then his study), even though it had happened over a hundred years ago. I'd established a connection with Sonja Lindholm, one of the archivists at the State Archives, who emailed me copies of the documents I requested from time to time, but searching for information about Captain Dusenberry's death beyond the scant mentions in military records and the local newspaper was pretty much a needle/haystack proposition.

I pulled up a PDF from Sonja's latest email and perused several dull letters about a charity concert held at the Exchange Hotel (now known as La Fonda) in 1884. Some of them mentioned Maria Hidalgo, whom I believed to have been in love with Captain Dusenberry, but only in passing among a list of subscribers to the concert.

The handwriting was more elegant than anything I could produce, and I'd always been proud of my penmanship. Something about the variation in thickness of the lines, probably a result of writing with a quill pen, made it exceptionally beautiful. Now cursive writing was no longer being taught in some schools. It might just be matter of time until only scholars would be able to read letters like these.

The digital age had its wonders, and also its costs.

I finished going through the PDF, finding nothing interesting. Sent an email to Sonja thanking her and asking for the next document on my list. Picked up my teacup and found it empty.

I stood and walked over to the credenza in Kris's office, where I always left the tea tray so that I'd have to get up to get more tea. Deciding to take a bit more of a break, I left my cup by the pot and went out into the hallway. Julio's salsa music was a muted distant thrumming beat, easily ignored in my office but more noticeable out here as it drifted up the stairwell.

The pitched roof of the old Victorian house gave the upstairs hallway a cathedral-ish ceiling. White sheers flanked the tall window at the western end, glowing softly in the indirect morning light. I remembered Vi standing before that window on the day she sang for a special tea in the main parlor downstairs. My throat tightened, recalling the happiness of that day and the sorrow that had followed. Such a promising artist, and dear friend, struck down so cruelly. I swallowed and walked through my little sitting area up to the window, looking down at my garden.

A few dry leaves skittered over the *portal's* roof below. The wisteria vines were starting to go yellow; the cottonwoods on the street were showing the first hint of gold. Autumn was a time of endings. Normally I loved it, but there was a hollow feeling in me today.

I went back to my office, poured tea, and picked up the phone, dialing Willow's number before I could procrastinate again. Two rings and she answered, her smooth voice intoning the name of her business.

"Willow, it's Ellen Rosings. Sorry it's taken me so long to get back to you."

"No problem, Ellen. I know you're busy."

There was a pause, and I thought I heard her take a long, slow breath.

"You wanted to talk about the tour and tea package for October?" I prompted.

"Ah...yes. Is this a good time?"

"Sure. I was thinking a light tea might be better than a full meal. A couple of savories, a scone, and one or two sweets. What do you think?"

"That sounds good. Yes, they'll probably only want to stay half an hour or so. Could the tea be served in the dining parlor?"

I grimaced. That room was where Captain Dusenberry had been murdered in the 19th century, and where Sylvia Carruthers had been murdered last spring. Some of my guests called it the "murder room," much to my dismay.

Perfectly understandable that Willow would want to finish her tour there. Captain Dusenberry was her grand finale, and the reason she was bringing groups of customers to my establishment. I gathered my manners about me and smiled, hoping it would reach my voice.

"Certainly, as long as there isn't already a reservation for the room."

"May I reserve it for the tour dates now?"

"Of course. What are they?"

She gave me a list of dates and times, and I entered them straight into our reservations calendar. Since the dining parlor was often empty, it gave me a warm feeling to book a dozen reservations, even if they were for light teas. Every customer in the tearoom was a potential sale in the gift shop on top of whatever refreshments they consumed, and hopefully they'd enjoy themselves enough to come back.

"And of course, Halloween," Willow said. "I'd like to do two tours that day if I may: one in the early afternoon, one in the evening."

"I can't give you Halloween night," I said. "There's a private party in the room from six p.m. on."

"What about late afternoon? Five?"

I thought about it. Kris had booked the room for a dinner with her Goth friends. They wouldn't actually sit down until closer to eight, but she needed time to decorate the room, and the kitchen staff would be busy cooking the dinner.

"Four would be better," I said.

"That'll work, if we can do the earlier one at one o'clock."

"Sure," I said, typing in the reservations.

"Just one more question: we talked about having a Civil War reenactor for some of the tours."

"Yes. I need to get a referral from Detective Aragón. I'll get back to you on that. Which tours would you want him for? You'll probably need to plan on an extra half hour..."

We nailed down the last few details, and Willow professed herself satisfied. "I'll call you with the numbers of each group two days in advance," she said. "Is that enough time?"

"Yes."

Silence stretched between us, making me wish I could see her face. I took a sip of tea. It had gone cold.

"Anything else I can help you with?" I said.

"No, that should do it," Willow said slowly. "Is there anything I can help *you* with?"

Surprised, I hesitated, trying to figure out what she meant. "No," I said. "Thanks."

"If you change your mind, call. Any time. I keep my cell with me."

"Um, thank you. I'll be in touch about the reenactor."

"I'll look forward to hearing from you. Take care, Ellen."

"You, too. Bye."

I put the phone down and frowned at it. What would Willow be able to help me with? What made her think I needed help?

She'd never made any claims of psychic abilities in our conversations, but her belief that ghosts—or spirits, as she always called them—were real was obvious, and some of her comments had implied at least some kind of sensitivity to them. I looked around my office, as if I might spot a recalcitrant spirit hanging about the corners of the sloped ceiling.

Captain Dusenberry had been quiet lately. I wondered if that was about to change.

Footsteps coming up the stairs at that moment made me catch my breath, but it was Julio, of course. He'd removed his baker's hat, setting his dark mop of curls loose.

"Done for the day?" I asked.

"Done with scones. I want to play around with the October savories after lunch. Should I make you something?"

"No, thanks. I have leftovers I need to use up."

"OK. I'll be back in about an hour, then." He nodded, then stared to one side for a moment, hands shoved in his pockets. "You'll be here?" he asked, looking up at me.

"Yes."

"Good. See you."

I watched him disappear down the stairs, then listened until he reached the ground floor and I heard the door open and shut. I closed my eyes, taking a deep breath. Relief at being alone flooded me, surprising in its strength. I hadn't realized how tense I was.

It must be from yesterday, I told myself.

My teapot was empty. I took it downstairs and put the kettle on. Rinsed the pot and infuser, spooned out fresh tea leaves. Wisteria White, this time; I needed the comfort.

While I waited for the kettle, I walked down the hall and looked into the parlors. Everything was tidy, ready for tomorrow. With the lights off and the alcoves empty, the tearoom seemed asleep, like Sleeping Beauty's castle, waiting to be awakened. I stood in the middle of the main parlor and slowly turned around, looking at each alcove—Jonquil, Iris, Rose, and Lily— and trying to summon a happy memory for each.

Laughing and joking with Gina and Nat as we painted and decorated. Delight on the faces of customers as they entered for the first time. Birthday celebrations, bridal showers, one memorable young couple who had planned a special tea together, each intending to propose to the other.

Darker memories came to me, too: the bittersweet recollection of Vi's voice filling this room with music, the peaceful but distressing demise of Maria Garcia—Julio and Rosa and Ramon's grandmother—in the Lily alcove, the time I crossed the street to take scones to a neighbor and was nearly strangled for my effort.

The kettle raised a distant whine, and I shook myself. Dust, these memories. Nothing more. Nothing I could change.

I returned to the pantry and turned off the kettle, letting it rest for a minute because I was brewing a white tea. Technically, I should have stayed to watch the kettle and caught it before it boiled, but since I was just brewing tea for myself I forgave myself for the lapse.

As I poured hot water over the tea leaves, the scents of currant and rose wafted up from the pot. Leaving it steeping, I stole into the kitchen to see what was in the fridge, and found two wisteria petit fours left over from Saturday. Julio would just throw them out because the icing would be a little stiff by Tuesday. He always made the cakes fresh.

I put the two orphans on a plate and set them on my tea tray along with the pot of Wisteria White. Climbing the stairs, I thought about what was in my own tiny fridge in my suite: chicken salad and some leftover marinara. I didn't feel like cooking pasta.

Life is short; eat dessert first. Who was it who said that?

I took the advice and ate the petit fours with a cup of hot tea while I surfed around on the Internet. Kris, my office manager, was always trying to get me to post things on social media sites. She had set up accounts for the tearoom and given me the logins, but I just didn't feel right tooting my own horn that way. I did check the pages now and then to see what Kris was posting on them.

Hints about special Halloween events in October were what she'd been posting, apparently, though I hadn't wanted to announce any details before finalizing the tour dates with Willow. Like Gina, Kris wanted me to capitalize on the tearoom's resident ghost as a marketing tool, though in Kris's case I think it was more a personal fascination with Captain Dusenberry than an interest in promoting the tearoom. She and her friends couldn't get enough of the dining parlor. They'd had dinners there twice, already, and for months had been making elaborate plans for Halloween night. Ramon was going to play the guitar, I knew.

They would have scorned a lecture from a Civil War reenactor, but they liked and respected Willow. It wouldn't have surprised me to learn that they'd invited her to join their dinner party.

Before I could forget about the reenactor, I got out my cell to send Tony a text.

> We need a Civil War reenactor for talks at the tearoom in October. Can you send a couple of phone numbers for me to try?

We'd talked about this possibility before, back when Tony had come dressed in a borrowed Civil War uniform to talk to Ramon and his friends (a somewhat less sophisticated group of Goths than Kris's set) about Captain Dusenberry. They'd all loved it, as had Willow, who had also been there.

I set the phone down, hoping for a return text. Nothing for ten minutes, while I surfed some more.

He was busy, no doubt. He had two murders to deal with, after all. A text from me was probably low-priority.

I disliked being low-priority.

Seeking distraction, I crossed the hall to my suite, dug out the chicken salad and some lettuce, and arranged them nicely on a plate. Rather than eat at my desk, I fetched my phone and sat in my sitting area by the front window.

The September sun wasn't yet shining in, but it would within the hour, and it was already warm upstairs. I opened the window a crack to let in some fresh air. A rustle of cottonwood leaves whispered in on the cool breeze. It made me want to run up into the mountains, where the aspens were starting to turn. Soon they would form the golden canopy under which I loved to walk every autumn, with the smell of dry leaves underfoot and the crisp, turquoise sky overhead.

Would Tony like to go on a picnic up there? Or would he think it too sentimental?

My pulse got a bit jittery at the thought. I really didn't know him all that well.

My phone buzzed its text noise. I grabbed it.

Sure.

I had to shake off the thought that he was accepting a picnic invitation and remind myself he was answering my request about the reenactor. Wanting more than a single syllable, I texted back at once, on the first topic I could think of.

I'm free Sunday night for a movie.

After waiting five minutes for a response, I returned to my computer to surf up some movies. I had promised a while ago—rather an embarrassing while ago—to go with Tony, but life had kept interfering with our plans. His schedule was unpredictable, and mine didn't mesh well with it. I was often too tired for much at the end of the work day, and lately a lot of my spare time had gone to planning Nat's wedding.

I chose a movie—a British social comedy that looked more smart than slapstick—and sent Tony another text with the title. This time I got an answer within a minute.

Not Sunday. Dinner with family.

He'd mentioned that once; dinner with his mother and grandmother every Sunday. I should have remembered.

Thursday, then?

No immediate response. Disappointed, I went back to sifting

through my messages.

I was on my third cup of tea and making a to-do list for the next day when I heard the back door open and close. It had to be Julio, but the salsa music didn't start up right away. Wondering if he'd left the door unlocked when he'd gone to lunch, I headed downstairs, and almost ran into him at the foot of the staircase.

"I was just coming to get you," he said. "Come see."

He led me toward the front of the tearoom, through the gift shop and back to the most secluded alcove, Violet. It had originally been Marigold, but I'd never liked the brown wing chairs (now reposing by the front door as a makeshift waiting area), and after Vi's death I had decided to rename it in her honor. We had changed the décor to varying shades of violet, with lace sheers between the window and the rich velvet curtains.

Julio stopped in the middle of the room and turned toward the fireplace. Hanging over the mantel, where I'd had a still-life of a bowl of marigolds, was a full-length portrait of Vi.

She was dressed in the lace and silk she'd worn when she sang in the main parlor. A background of dark purple draperies emphasized the brightness of her form. She held a small bouquet of violets in one hand, from which one bloom had fallen to the floor, a nice touch. Her smile shone out from the canvas, and her hair was a burnished crown, catching glints of almost otherworldly light. The tone of the painting was soft and glowing, reminding me of my favorite pre-Raphaelite artists.

"I finished it this weekend," Julio said in a low voice.

"It's beautiful," I said, and burst into tears.

4

JULIO TURNED TO ME, concern tightening the classic Latin lines of his face. "I'm sorry, Boss. I didn't mean to upset you."

I shook my head, wanting to say that I wasn't upset, except that the deep sobs rising up in me prevented my speaking. It wasn't just Vi; it was everything. The portrait had tipped me over the edge of a precipice, and all my pent-up grief and stress were spilling out.

"Why don't you sit down a minute? I can bring you some tea."

If I'd had any breath to spare, I'd have laughed at the picture of my coffee-aligned chef making tea. It was a kind thought, and I acknowledged it the only way I could, by taking his advice and sitting in one of the violet wing chairs.

He left, and I struggled to control my weeping. My inability to do so worried me. I rubbed at my eyes; no handkerchief at hand, and the nearest tissue was in the restroom. I took a long, shuddering breath, then hiccuped.

Really, that's enough, I told myself.

Myself didn't pay any attention. The tears flowed on, and while I managed to cry without moaning, I still couldn't stop.

Voices sounded in the hallway. I thought an unladylike word, and tried to rub my face into order.

A delivery? I hoped Julio would get rid of whoever it was.

Footsteps striding closer. It was not my day.

"This isn't a good time," I heard Julio say from the gift shop.

"Won't take but a minute," drawled a familiar voice. "She back here?"

Desperate to control myself, I held my breath. Hiccuped again, which hurt.

Detective Walters came in, his tall form a looming presence in the cozy alcove. At least he had taken off his cowboy hat, which he held in one hand. Julio entered on his heels like an angry spaniel, and reached around him to hand me a box of tissue.

I drew breath to thank him, and hiccuped.

"Like I said, not a good time," Julio said, moving to stand by my chair.

"Sorry to see you upset, ma'am," said Walters, with no detectable sympathy. "Hope nothing bad's happened."

Mopping at my face with a handful of tissue, I shook my head. Julio just stared resentfully at Walters, which did nothing to ease the awkwardness.

I took a few deep breaths and finally managed to speak, in a rather soggy voice. "Nothing's happened. Not lately, anyway." Hiccup.

I pulled another tissue from the box, waved it in the direction of Julio's painting, then blew my nose.

"That a friend of yours?" said Walters, gazing at the portrait.

"She used to work here," Julio said, his voice cold. "She died a few months ago."

"Julio painted her portrait—hic—and he just hung it up," I said. "It brought back some memories."

"Hm," said Walters. "Well, I'm sorry to come at a bad time. Just thought you'd want to know the results of the autopsy on Mr. Swazo. He died from a ruptured kidney."

I looked up at him. "Kidney?" Hiccup.

The detective's gaze was sharp and steady. Looking for me to betray something, I figured, but there was nothing to betray.

"Yeah," he said, still watching me. "Must've happened during the beating."

"What beating?" Julio said, looking alarmed. "What's this about?"

Walters turned to him. "Your boss didn't tell you that she found a body yesterday?"

Julio's eyes widened as he turned to me. "Another one?"

"No, I didn't tell him," I said, annoyed at his response,

though by now Walters must know of the other investigations I'd been involved in. "I'd like to forget about it, to be honest. Was there anything else you—hic—needed?"

I stood up, to encourage Walters to leave. Three of us standing in the alcove made rather a crowd, and both men edged back to give me more room.

"No, ma'am. Just thought I'd let you know that it's officially a murder investigation."

"Well, I hope you find the k—hic—killer."

I led them out, still clutching my box and a wad of sodden tissue. Without pausing I walked straight to the back entrance, thanked the detective for coming (not very sincerely), and shut the door behind him. Then hiccuped.

"Sorry, boss," Julio said. "I meant to get rid of him, but when I opened the door he just came in."

"It's all right, Julio. Thanks for the—hic—tissue."

"Let me get you a glass of water."

I followed him into the kitchen, sat at the break table, and drank the water he brought me. Still sniffling and hiccuping, I thanked him for Vi's portrait.

"It's perfect," I said. "You really have a gift. Why on earth did you—hic—choose cooking instead of painting?"

"Better shot at making a living," he said with a shrug and a fleeting grimace.

"But less chance of becoming a star. You could, you know. You're that talented. Hic."

He got up and refilled the water glass, brought it back to me. "This time drink from the far edge. No," he added as I turned the glass around in my hands. "You'll have to stand up, and you'll probably get wet. Put your mouth on the far edge of the glass, lean forward, and drink at least half of the water at once."

I obeyed. Straightening, I wiped my chin. "Well, at least I'll be hydrated."

"What did that cop mean about another body?"

I sat down and told him about finding Swazo in Nat's driveway. Julio listened, his frown deepening as I explained how

I'd seen the victim at the flea market in the morning.

"That's not good."

"No, well. Worse for him than for me."

"Why would he follow you to Nat's house?"

"He didn't follow us. It's a coincidence. The road is right there."

"I don't like it."

"Well, neither do—hic—I. Dammit."

"Maybe you should take a nap."

I sighed. "I'll try. Thanks, Julio."

"See you tomorrow, boss."

I went upstairs, holding my breath and hiccuping twice. Stepped into my office to get my phone and check for messages. Sonja had sent me the next file from the archives. No text from Tony.

I doubted that I'd be able to sleep; I rarely slept during daylight hours, usually only when I was ill. Also, hiccups.

A bath might help me relax. I went into my suite, locked the door, and ran a hot bath, adding some scented salts that Gina had given me. My second bath in as many days. What decadence!

I got in, leaned back, and tried to let the hot water soak away my cares. The hiccups kept interfering. Yet again, I tried holding my breath, without success. When the water had gone tepid I gave up and toweled off, then put on some sweats even thought it wasn't quite five. I was taking the rest of the day off.

My phone rang as I was brushing out my hair. It was my aunt.

"Nat! Sorry, I forgot to call you!" I curled up in my armchair by the chimney.

"That's all right, dear. Are you joining us for dinner?"

I looked out the window. Wind was stirring the leaves of the trees. I hiccuped.

"Honestly, I think I'd rather stay home tonight. Sorry."

"That's OK, honey. There's plenty of time. Are you feeling all right?"

"Well, I've had the hiccups all afternoon."

"Oh, dear! Have you tried lemon and sugar?"

"No. You mean—hic—in tea?"

"No, no. Sprinkle some sugar on a slice of lemon, then bite it and suck on it until the sugar's all gone. Works every time for me."

"Thanks. I'll try that."

"How are you otherwise? Did Detective Walters call you?"

"No, he came in person. Did you get a visit?"

"Just a call."

"Hm. Wonder why I r—hic—rate. Maybe I'm the prime suspect."

"Now you know that's ridiculous! I was with you all day."

"You could be a co-conspirator."

"Oh, Ellen—I worry when you get cynical like this."

"Sorry. Guess I'm a little down today. Julio finished his portrait of Vi and hung it up in the Violet alcove. It's—hic—really gorgeous, but it brought all that back to me."

"Did you ever talk to that nice counselor?"

"No."

"Maybe you should give him a call."

A gust of wind slapped the window. I hugged my knees.

"Maybe. I'll think about it."

"All right, dear. Well, you feel better. I'll be in tomorrow."

Nat didn't usually work Tuesdays. I bit back an urge to tell her not to come. It was her mother hen instinct; I had to respect that. I ought to be grateful for her concern.

"Thanks," I said. "I'll try the lemon thing."

We said goodbye and I debated whether to just go to bed. The hiccups convinced me to at least try Nat's remedy. I didn't have any lemons upstairs, but we always had them downstairs, for lemon curd. On the way, I grabbed the tea tray from my office.

"Julio?" I said at the foot of the stairs, self-conscious about my sweats.

No answer, and no salsa music. I advanced into the kitchen

and found it empty, quickly washed the tea things and left them drying in the rack, then grabbed a lemon and scooted back upstairs to wash it and cut a slice. I sprinkled a liberal dose of sugar on it, then bit down on it.

Oh, the sour! I mmphed a protest but sucked as instructed. When the sugar was gone and only the sour remained, I spat it out. And hiccuped.

"Ugh!"

I rinsed my mouth and drank some water, feeling queasy. What I wanted was tea.

I put my kettle on and took out my personal pot, an old favorite that happened to be violet chintz. While the tea was brewing I checked my phone for texts. Nothing from Tony, but there was one from Gina:

> Dinner 2nite?

I hiccuped. Frowning, I texted back:

> No, I have the hiccups.

> Eat some ice cream.

> Right.

> Srsly, it helps. Peppermint if u have it.

> OK. Thanks.

I had no peppermint ice cream. I had no ice cream at all, and I was not going out to get some. I was staying home. Perhaps crawling under a rock.

The timer went off and I poured myself a cup of tea, returning to my armchair to nurse it. The daylight was fading, and the wind had diminished a little. I thought about dinner, but felt uninspired. I ended up making cinnamon toast and curling up with a book until I was sleepy enough to go to bed.

The hiccups were still with me. I slept fitfully, troubled by unsettling dreams that I couldn't remember. I got up and tried

Julio's wrong-side-of-the-glass thing again, but it didn't help. Finally I dozed off out of sheer exhaustion.

I was walking along a dirt road somewhere near the Opera. I could hear someone singing an aria, a beautiful mezzo-soprano, and I wondered if it was Vi. I walked faster, hoping to get to the opera house before the music ended, but a man stood in my way. He was Indian, with dark eyes fixed intently on mine. He held up a folded knife, the hilt striped with sugilite and turquoise. He was not threatening me with it, just showing it to me, but the sight of it frightened me and I screamed.

I sat up, trembling, heart pounding. I was sure I had actually screamed. The man in the dream was Daniel Swazo.

Rubbing my face, I sighed. Then hiccuped.

I flung out of bed, angry at the universe. Stood under a hot shower until the trembling had ceased, then pulled on my sweats again and looked at the time.

4:42. Too early to start the day, and probably too late to get any more meaningful sleep. Besides, I didn't want to go back to that dream.

I wandered out into the hallway and over to the window. A gibbous moon was setting behind the houses across the street. I stared at it, and realized that I was crying again.

I sat in my mother's overstuffed armchair and wept and hiccuped until the tears ended. Maybe Nat was right; maybe I should call the counselor who had come to help the tearoom staff cope with Vi's murder.

Loren something. Very handsome in an otherworldly, almost angelic way. Very gentle and kind. I'd avoided him. I had told him—and myself—that I wasn't ready to talk. But maybe I had really been afraid.

Afraid of what, though? I couldn't answer that question.

Seeking distraction, I went to my computer and pulled up the file that Sonja had sent me. This one was a set of letters belonging to the post doctor at Fort Marcy. They were letters he had received; no copies of the letters he had written, so they represented a rather disjointed correspondence. Mostly boring, but one note written in a flourishing, somewhat uncontrolled hand caught my attention:

Father,

Mrs H. informs me she saw Capt. D. tete-a-tete with that Spanish woman at the concerto. I see now that you were Right to Caution me, and I will heed your Wisdom henceforth. I have no hope of the Capt. now as Mrs H says his attentions to the Spaniard were Quite Pointed. I shall devote myself to my Studies with the Sisters.

Your obedient,

Lucy

Lucy sounded more bitter than obedient, but maybe my interpretation was colored by my own mood. More important was the fact that the note seemed to confirm my suspicion: Captain Dusenberry had been in love with Maria Hidalgo.

I still had the captain's letters from Maria locked in my desk. They did not mention love, but the tone was warm and affectionate. Lucy's note supported my surmise, and also showed that others in the community had noticed.

Whites and Hispanics had intermarried in the 19th century. It was by no means uncommon, but Maria came from a family of Spanish aristocrats who had, I believed, opposed her wish to marry a white man. Captain Dusenberry had rank and importance, but was not an aristocrat.

The question was, had Maria's family felt so strongly about her friendship with the captain that they had murdered him to prevent their marrying?

I brought up my file of notes on the captain's murder and

added a line about Lucy's letter. Going back to the beginning of the file, I looked for any mention of the type of gun used to kill the captain.

There it was: a Colt Navy revolver. Willow had told me about it, when she'd given me the details about the murder. She'd said it was a common sidearm, which was discouraging, but if there was any way to find out who had owned such a weapon, that might lead to the captain's killer.

I wrote a short email to Bennett Cole at the Museum of New Mexico, asking if he could help me find out who in Santa Fe had owned Colt Navy revolvers in 1855. Maybe it was a silly question, but I had to try.

Frowning at my screen without seeing the text, I mulled over the problem. Willow had said the Navy revolver was favored by the military, which implied the killer had been a soldier. That made sense, since most of the people the captain had associated with would have been military.

But civilians owned them, too. Maybe one of the Hidalgos had owned one.

I wrote a quick email to Sonja at the archives, asking her to do a search on Hidalgo and Colt Navy revolver. A little hum of excitement went through me as I sent it off.

I hiccuped.

Cursing softly, I went back to my suite and got dressed. The sky outside was lightening. It was still early, but Julio would be arriving soon, and in case he came up to check on me I didn't want to be sitting around in my nightclothes.

I should eat breakfast, too, though the hiccups made me less interested in eating. I put the kettle on, then made soft-boiled eggs and toast, and sliced up an orange. My nightmare kept returning to my thoughts. Did Daniel Swazo want something from me?

Could ghosts visit our dreams? I could ask Willow, but I suspected I knew what she would say, and I was pretty sure I didn't want to hear it.

I heard the door downstairs, followed by Julio's music, very quiet; if I'd been asleep I wouldn't have noticed it. He didn't come up.

When I'd finished my breakfast and cleaned up the dishes, I poured myself a fresh cup of tea and returned to my office. The aroma of something baking—cake for the petit fours, probably—drifted up the stairwell. I sat at my desk, took a deep breath, and looked through my stash of miscellaneous business cards. The one I wanted had a blue and white picture of a dove flying upward. I laid it on the center of my desk.

Loren Jackson, counselor. The business name was Hospice Center.

A glance at my clock told me it was too early to call; 6:20. I wrote an email, very short and businesslike, thanking him again for the help he had given my staff in the summer, and asking for an appointment. I sent it off before I could chicken out.

Having committed, I put away the card and turned my attention to messages. I had actually dealt with them all and run out of things to do by the time Kris arrived. She stepped through the doorway that our offices shared and looked in on me. Her outfit du jour was a black knit dress that hugged her figure, black accent scarf with beaded fringe, and black knee-high boots. I wondered if she'd been raiding Willow's wardrobe.

"Morning," she said. "Is there tea?"

"Um—I probably drank it all. I'll make some more. Hic."

Her brows rose. "Hiccups, eh?"

"Yeah." I stood and picked up the tea tray.

"Pull your tongue."

"Beg pardon?"

"Pull your tongue. It'll make them stop. Try it."

I suspected Miss Manners would say that tongue-pulling should be done in private, so I carried the tray downstairs and put on a kettle, then slipped into the restroom to give it a try. Apart from making whatever ligaments or muscles connected the bottom of my tongue to my jaw sore, it had no effect.

Giving up, I took my violet chintz teapot into the kitchen to wash it. Julio glanced up at me from a work table covered in flour. I smiled back and hiccuped.

"Still?" he said.

"Uh-huh."

I turned on the high-power hose at the commercial dishwashing station and blasted the teapot until it sparkled, then took it back to the pantry and pondered over what tea to make. I'd already had Darjeeling, so I picked a blended black with flower petals and grapefruit peel, hoping the citrus would perk me up. It was going to be a challenge to get through the day without dragging. I already felt tired.

In high school, I'd sometimes stayed up all night playing cards or other games. In college I'd pulled all-nighters cramming for tests, and I still got caught by a book occasionally and stayed up too late reading, but nowadays I couldn't do it without feeling the impact. I could try for an afternoon nap, but the activity in the tearoom would only make it harder to sleep during the day. Maybe I'd go to bed early.

Iz came in while I was waiting for the tea to steep, wearing the lavender dress that was the tearoom servers' uniform. "Morning, Ellen," she said in her soft voice, and a falling note in her tone made me look closely at her.

"Good morning. Everything all right?"

She was quiet for a moment as she put on her Victorian style apron. "Pretty much," she said finally, tying the strings.

She wasn't the sort of person who goes around smiling all the time, but she was usually pretty centered, and seemed less so than normal. I wondered if something was going on at home. She still lived with her folks at Tesuque Pueblo...

Oh.

"Did you know Daniel Swazo?" I asked gently.

5

Iz SWALLOWED AND BLINKED. "Not well. He was a year ahead of me in school." She looked straight at me then. "How did you know?"

I stifled a sigh. No sense putting it off; she'd find out sooner or later.

"I found his body. He was in Nat's driveway."

Her eyes went wide. "What was he doing there?"

"I wish I knew."

She looked away, taking a teapot down from the shelf and setting it on the counter. A frown creased her brow. "I heard he got beat up."

She shot me a questioning glance. I nodded.

"I'm sorry, Iz. If you—hic—want to take the day off..."

"No, I'm all right. I'm sorry for *you*, finding him like that."

"Thanks."

"It must be hard. You already found Mrs. Carruthers, and Julio's grandma, and Vi..."

My timer went off, saving me from having to answer. I took the tea upstairs, poured some for Kris, and went to my office, where a new set of messages that Kris had peeled off the voicemail awaited me. I added sugar to my own cup of tea and glanced through them, then fetched my phone from my suite, checking for texts. There were none. I returned to my desk, feeling cross.

I had not, in fact, found Julio's grandmother's body. It was Rosa, another of my servers who was also her granddaughter, who found her peacefully passed in the Lily alcove, where she had been having tea. Of course, Rosa had summoned me at once, and I'd called 911, and all the rest had ensued.

If nothing else, I was getting good at the drill.

I turned to my computer to check my email. There was a message from Loren Jackson. I hiccuped.

> *Good to hear from you, Ellen. I'd be happy to talk with you. I have an opening at 2:00 today. Can you come to the Center, or should I come to the tearoom?*

My first instinct was to answer that today wouldn't do, but considering the fact that I'd caught up on my messages for the first time in I didn't know how long—maybe ever—that excuse seemed lame even to me. Also, I was heartily tired of the hiccups. Maybe he'd be able to recommend a solution that did not involve eating, drinking, or pulling on parts of myself.

I took a bracing swallow of tea, then wrote back saying that 2:00 would be fine.

"Kris," I said, stepping into her office, "I've got an appointment this afternoon. You don't have me booked for any—hic—thing, do you?"

"No. Did you try pulling your tongue?"

"Yes. No luck."

"Maybe you didn't pull it hard enough."

"If I'd pulled any harder, I wouldn't be talking to you now. Hic. More tea?"

"I'm good. Thanks."

I poured more for myself and went back to my desk, where I worked my way through the new messages, then surfed up the location of the Hospice Center. It was out on Rodeo Road, on the south side of town. I decided to go early and grab some lunch on the way. There was a little family-owned place that specialized in soups, with a Hungarian mushroom soup that I couldn't get enough of.

Plans in place, desk cleared of messages, I had an hour to kill. It was just before eleven, when we opened for business, so I went downstairs to check on the tearoom and be ready to greet the guests.

Nat was coming in the back door as I reached the ground floor. She cast a worried glance at me, then smiled.

"Good morning, Ellen. How are you feeling?"

"Morning, Nat." I gave her a hug. "I'm fine. Hic."

"Oh, sweetheart! Did you try the lemon?"

"I did. Let's go to the gift shop."

I led the way down the hall, a bit briskly. In the gift shop I fired up the register and brought up the reservations page. It was a new system and I was still getting used to it, a step up from the paper printouts we had used at first. I had balked at the expense, but Kris had been right: the electronic system saved us a lot of back and forth and made everything run more smoothly. Guests could even book their own reservations online.

I saw that we had three parties booked for 11:00, including Mrs. Olafssen—the Bird Woman—with a group of six. Gritting my teeth, I made up my mind to say hello to her. She was a regular, one of our best customers. I had also come to view her as my own personal karmic challenge. I was determined to be nice to her no matter what she said or did.

Glancing at the clock, I saw that we had a few minutes before opening. "Come in here, Nat," I said, heading through Hyacinth toward Violet.

I stood in front of the fireplace and looked up at Julio's portrait of Vi. Sadness stirred beneath my heart, but I managed to keep from crying.

"Oh," Nat said in a reverent tone. "It's lovely. He captured her smile perfectly."

"Yes," I said, my throat tightening.

Nat slid her arm around my waist and hugged. "What a wonderful tribute."

I nodded and brushed away a stray tear, then inhaled deeply. I was not going to lose it again, I told myself.

I hiccuped, and swore under my breath.

Nat squeezed me. "Why don't you take the day off, dear? Go up to Ten Thousand Waves."

I imagined hiccuping my way through a massage. "Maybe

tomorrow. I made an appointment to see that counselor this afternoon."

"Oh, good! I liked him. He's a good listener."

"He ought to be. It's his job."

I went back out to the gift shop, where I found Dee Gallagher, another of my servers, putting price labels on some whimsical, leaf-shaped tea strainers. Dee had a good eye for what little trinkets the customers might like, and I'd put her in charge of finding new items for the gift shop, subject to my approval and the constraints of our budget.

"Morning, Ellen," she said, smiling and brushing a strand of blonde hair behind her ear.

"Good morning. You were right, those are charming."

"Thanks! They make some pumpkin-shaped ones, too. If these sell well, maybe we could order some of the pumpkins for next month."

"Mm."

I didn't want to go overboard with the seasonal items. The gift shop was pretty full already, with tea and tea accessories and a few miscellaneous items. We didn't have space to go wild with hats and gloves and china and a lot of the other things Dee had suggested. At some point, I might consider expanding, but not until the mortgage balance was a lot smaller.

I crossed the hall to the main parlor and visited each of the parties there. The Bird Woman and four of her cronies had taken over the Rose alcove, and from their attire I gathered it was a meeting of the Red Hat Society. The Bird Woman wore a scarlet dress with a ruffled neckline so fluffy it reminded me of a Thanksgiving turkey. Her hat would have challenged Scarlett O'Hara.

They were already tucking into their tea so I merely paused to smile and wish them a good morning, but despite having a full mouth the Bird Woman stopped me from escaping with a frantic wave. Her eyes were sparrow-bright beneath the brim of her hat.

"It's nice to see you again, Mrs. Olafssen," I said, giving her time to swallow.

She took a large gulp of tea and sighed. "Heard you found another one!"

"Pardon?"

"Another deader."

I took a short, sharp breath, but managed to maintain my smile. Iz must have mentioned it, was all I could think. I picked up the teapot and poured the last of the tea into the Bird Woman's cup.

"I'm afraid the police don't want me—hic—to discuss it."

"You're turning into a regular corpse-magnet," she said gleefully.

"I'll just get you a fresh pot."

It was all I could do to keep from running down the hall to the butler's pantry. Iz was there, setting up a three-tiered food tray.

"Rose needs more tea," I said, putting the pot on the counter. I didn't wait for her to answer, but darted upstairs.

Purse, phone, keys, shades, light jacket against the breeze that was stirring up the first fallen leaves. I looked in on Kris, who was typing intently.

"Going out to lunch," I said, "and then my appointment. Hic."

She nodded, still typing. I went downstairs, donned my shades, and slipped out the back door.

A cool breeze greeted me, scented with a hint of autumn leaves. I paused to take a deep breath, and felt tension drain from my shoulders. I looked back at the house, feeling sad. I *loved* my tearoom. I shouldn't need to escape it.

I hiccuped.

I got in the car and backed out of the driveway, rolling down the window in the hope of catching more of that lovely autumn smell. It wasn't the tearoom that was the problem. It was everything else. I had multiple stressors.

I drove to the soup place and ordered a big bowl of mushroom soup, and shamelessly gobbled the baguette slices that came with it. Fortunately, I didn't have time to indulge in dessert as well.

The Hospice Center was a small storefront in a smallish shopping center. Unpretentious. No frills. The woman at the front desk gave me a motherly smile when I came in and told her my name.

I sat in one of three lime green plastic chairs in the waiting area, glanced at a side table of magazines, and took out my phone to shut it off. There was a text waiting; I hadn't noticed when it came in. It was from Tony.

> Sorry 4 late answer. Working case. Thursday out. Sorry.

Damn.

Even more terse than usual, which probably meant he was working around the clock on this one. I sighed and turned off the phone.

"Ellen?"

The voice was soft and warm. Loren Jackson came toward me, a friendly smile on his face. He wore a button-down shirt and casual slacks, but somehow still contrived to look elegant, perhaps because of his ethereal coloring. Pale hair brushed his eyebrows, and fine lines crinkled beside his blue eyes as he smiled.

"It's good to see you." The hand he offered was as warm as his voice. "Come on back."

I followed him down a narrow hallway. Expecting an office, I was surprised when we walked into a lounge with a comfy sofa and armchairs around a coffee table, a round cafe table that would seat four, and a kitchenette with a stovetop and coffee maker. The coffee actually smelled good.

"Please make yourself comfortable. Would you like coffee? I hesitate to offer you tea, though we have some teabags."

"Coffee would be great, thanks." I chose one of the overstuffed armchairs, and sank into it with a sigh.

"Cream and sugar?"

"Just cream."

Loren brought me a steaming mug and sat in another chair at right angles to mine. I caught a whiff of his cologne—something evergreenish—as he settled. "How are things at the tearoom?"

"Oh, well...not bad."

He sipped his coffee. I sipped mine. It wasn't as good as Julio's, but it was decent. A cut above the average office coffee.

"Julio painted a wonderful portrait of Vi," I said, wrapping my hands around the mug to let the heat soak into my fingers. "I got a little overwhelmed when I—hic—saw it. That's why I called you. I'd been meaning to talk to you about her and just never found the time."

His gentle smile bloomed and he nodded. "Well, I'm glad you found the time now. Tell me about the portrait."

I described it to him, and then told him about the day Vi sang at the tearoom, and how the memory of it had made me cry when Julio brought in the painting. I got a little watery talking about it, but managed to keep it together. The coffee table had a box of tissue on it, fortunately. When I pulled one to tidy my face, he spoke.

"How long have you had the hiccups?"

"Since yesterday after—hic—noon. And yes, I've tried a number of remedies."

"What set them off?"

I had to think about it. "I was crying over the portrait, and then Detective Walters came, and I guess I got a little stressed."

"Detective Walters?" Loren asked.

So I told him about finding Daniel Swazo, and the investigation, and how Walters had come to the tearoom just when I was going to pieces over Vi. He listened attentively, a tiny frown creasing his brow.

"Well, you've certainly had a lot to deal with," he said when I ran down. "You know, hiccups can be triggered by stress."

"They can?"

He nodded. "You might want to talk to your doctor about it, if they continue."

"Is there something that can be prescribed?"

"I don't know, but I'm not a doctor. I do know that getting plenty of rest, and minimizing the stresses in your life, can help."

"Have you had other—hic—clients with hiccups?"

He nodded again, looking grave.

"What's the longest attack you've heard about?"

"The longest I've seen first-hand was about two weeks."

"Two *weeks?*"

"I've heard of longer. But don't worry about that. Focus on what you can control. Can others help you out at the tearoom? Take some of the burden off you?"

"It's not that the tearoom's a burden. My staff is great, really. It's just that everything's sort of piling up at once."

"Mm. Can you get away for a couple of days? Go up to Ojo Caliente maybe?"

"The spa? I've never been there. Isn't it expensive?"

"Doesn't have to be. The day pass is reasonable, and gets you into all the public pools. If you've never been there I recommend it. They have a great restaurant, too."

I sipped my coffee, musing. I hadn't had a vacation since the tearoom had opened. Well, since I'd bought the building, really. More than a year ago.

Maybe a weekend...

The thought of inviting Tony slid through my mind and my cheeks flushed hot. I buried my face in my coffee mug, embarrassed.

Loren seemed not to notice. When I glanced up at him, he was looking at his phone. He met my gaze and flashed a smile.

"Sorry—I know it's rude. I just thought I'd check to see if there was a special at Ojo. They run them now and then, and it can save you some money."

"Thanks. I'll think about that. It's true that I'd enjoy a break." I shot another glance at him. "Have you stayed there?"

He nodded. "Not as often as I'd like, but yes. The quiet is amazing."

Quiet sounded really good. Not that my life was particularly noisy, but it was busy.

If the tearoom were all I had to deal with, I'd have been fine. But add in murder investigations—multiple—and it was getting overwhelming.

I swallowed the last of my coffee and set down my mug.

"More?" Loren offered.

"No thanks. Hic. Can I ask you a question?"

"Absolutely."

"Do you...talk about dreams much? Is that part of your work?"

He smiled. "I talk about whatever you want. If you mean do I interpret dreams, only in a haphazard way. I'm not trained in it, though I've done some reading."

"I had a dream...well, a nightmare. I saw the man I found. Daniel Swazo. He was showing me a knife."

"He was alive?"

"Yes. Well...yes."

"Did he look...forgive me..."

"Like he did when I found him? No. He looked like he did at the flea market, only more intense. He stared at me and showed me the—hic—knife, like it was important somehow."

"Was he threatening you?"

"No, the knife was folded shut."

"Hm. Any idea what the knife could signify? He wasn't stabbed, was he?"

"No."

Victor Solano was—and he was another murder victim that I hadn't found. But that had been last summer, and except for selling his wares within a mile of the Opera, I didn't think Swazo had any connection to Solano.

I had a feeling the knife wasn't important as a weapon, but beyond that I had no clue what Daniel Swazo had been trying to tell me.

"Can you tell me what the knife looked like?" Loren asked.

"Just a folding knife, like a pocket knife. The handle was decorated with colored stone, kind of in a mosaic. Swazo sold knives like that at the flea market."

"So he was showing you his work."

"Yeeaah...but not like showing it off."

He hadn't shown off the knives at his table. He'd let me look at them myself. Why, then, had he held the knife up in his fist in my dream? As if to say, *This is important*.

But why?

I shook my head. "I don't know. It doesn't make sense."

"Had you seen the knife he was showing you before? At the flea market."

"No." I frowned trying to picture the knife again. Irregular stripes of turquoise, malachite, sugilite...

I sat up straighter. "Yes I had seen it. In my aunt's driveway." I looked at Loren and the care in his blue eyes made me catch my breath.

"Detective Walters showed it to me, in an evidence bag. They found it in the driveway."

"Where Swazo was," Loren said.

I nodded.

"So it was his own knife, not a piece he was selling."

"I guess so."

"Do you think he was coming to show it to you?"

"When he died? No."

Loren put his mug on the table and leaned back in his chair, hands resting on his knees. He tilted his head a little to one side. "It's just an interesting coincidence."

I bit down on my annoyance. "Well, Detective Walters would agree with you, but it *is* a coincidence. He had no reason to follow us. It was hours after we'd seen him. That he came up Nat's driveway was just...bad luck."

Loren nodded, accepting my assessment. "I wonder why he would want to show you his knife."

"Me too." I glanced at my watch, and sighed. "I'd better get back. Thanks for your time."

"You're welcome. Come back any time."

I collected my purse and stood. "Do I pay the receptionist?"

"There's no charge. Our grief counseling services are underwritten by a grant."

"Oh! Well, then, may I make a donation? You did so much good for my staff."

He rose and picked up our coffee mugs, a smile quirking up one corner of his mouth. "If you like. I'll get you a brochure."

I'd had brochures, once. He'd left a stack of them when he visited the tearoom. I hadn't done more than glance at them.

He took one from a display on the counter and handed it to me. "I'm glad you came."

"Thanks. Me too. Hic."

"I hope those go away. Do try to get some rest."

I nodded. "Thanks for the idea about Ojo. Maybe I'll go up for a weekend."

"The rooms cost more on weekends, unfortunately."

"Perils of a day job," I said, trying for a light tone.

He smiled, but there was a hint of concern on his face. Nice of him to care.

Feeling self-conscious, I headed toward the lobby. Loren followed me down the hall and opened the front door.

"It was good to see you," he said.

I turned and was startled anew at the intense blue of his eyes. His gaze was also intense; he seemed about to say something, then instead smiled and offered a hand.

"Take care, Ellen."

I shook hands. Warm touch, and again a whisper of evergreen and spice.

"Thanks. You, too."

As I drove to the tearoom, I thought back over our conversation. Something was niggling at me about Daniel Swazo's knife. I hadn't connected the knife in the dream to the knife in the evidence bag before. Assuming it was my subconscious and not actually Swazo's ghost that was trying to tell me something, what did it mean?

I reached no conclusions by the time I pulled into my parking space behind the house. For a minute I sat looking through the windshield at the French doors of the dining parlor and the sheers beyond them. I felt reluctant to go in, and that bothered me.

I hiccuped. Swearing softly, I picked up my purse and went inside.

"There you are!" said Nat, coming down the hall toward me. "Dee was looking for you."

"Is she in the gift shop?"

"No, I've been watching it until just now. I was going to take a quick break." She nodded in the direction of the restroom.

"I'll go watch until you're—hic—back."

A couple of customers were browsing in the gift shop. I put my purse under the counter and stayed by the register, hoping that the Bird Woman wouldn't come in. She must surely have left by now, I told myself.

I was ringing up a sale of some packaged tea and one of Dee's leaf tea-strainers when Nat came back. She stepped in beside me as the customer departed.

"Dee's in the pantry. She asked me to send you back."

"OK. Thanks."

I grabbed my purse as Nat smiled at another customer coming up to the counter. The sound of guests conversing in the main parlor followed me down the hall and into the little side hallway that led to the restrooms, the butler's pantry, and the kitchen. I stepped into the pantry, but no one was there. Intending to check the kitchen, I turned.

"Hah!"

A looming figure jumped toward me from the doorway. I flinched back and gave a little shriek, then recovered.

"Mick Gallagher, what on earth do you think you're doing?!"

My dish washer transformed from a monster into a puppy dog, one wisp of blonde hair escaped from his pony tail and hanging beside his face, brown eyes wide and looking slightly hurt. "Just trying to help with your hiccups," he said.

Dee stepped into the doorway beside her brother. "It was my idea. Did it work?"

I closed my eyes and drew a breath. "I appreciate the thought, but I'm fine, really. Hic."

"Aww," said Mick.

"Please *don't* try again."

They yielded to me as I went out and into the kitchen. Julio glanced up at me from his work table and grinned.

"Don't start," I said.

"I told them it was a bad idea."

"Everything all right here? I'm going upstairs."

"I'm good. Need a couple of grocery items, but it's not urgent. I put a note on your desk."

I breezed past the pantry, where Mick and Dee were talking in low tones, and hurried upstairs. First stop was my suite, to drop off my purse and put the kettle on for tea, because I was *not* going back down to the pantry. While I waited for it to boil I checked my phone, then stepped across to Kris's office.

"How was your appointment?" she asked, looking up at me.

"Great. Very helpful. Hic."

She gazed steadily at me, as if deciding how to handle me. "Want your messages?" she said at last.

I stepped forward to accept them, then went into my office to drop them on my desk and collect the tea tray, which I carried back to my suite. Brewing tea was a soothing task, and the aroma of Darjeeling made me relax a little.

I was almost out of loose tea, though. I'd have to raid the pantry...after the staff had gone home.

Returning to my office, I poured myself a fresh cup and offered some to Kris, then settled at my desk. Julio's grocery list was short: lemons and pumpkins ("FRESH"). I wondered what he was planning. Every restaurant and fast food chain did pumpkin this time of year, and I wasn't inclined to follow the trend. Pumpkin scones? Pumpkin curd? No.

A short stack of mail sat next to my messages: two business letters and a cream-colored envelope from Nat. Her wedding invitation.

I opened it, smiling at the somewhat less than formal text

inviting me and a guest to attend the wedding of Natasha Wheeler and Manuel Sanchez. My stomach clenched at the thought of inviting Tony. That's who Nat expected me to bring.

Would he consider an invitation to escort me a wedding to be rather pointed? I didn't want to give him the wrong idea. Or rather, the right idea with the wrong emphasis.

Maybe I should just ignore the question, and go stag.

Saturday would help me decide, when Tony brought his mother and grandmother to tea. *If* he brought them to tea. I wondered if his case would keep him away. I pulled up the reservations software and checked; his reservation hadn't been canceled.

I turned my attention to the lavender message sheets. A call from Gina, no message. A response from Bennett Cole at the museum, asking me to call back about the Colt Navy revolvers. A reminder from Willow about the reenactor.

I checked my phone, but there were no new messages or texts. Should I text Tony again? I hated to bother him if he was really tied up in his case, but I did need to pin down the reenactor before too much longer.

My desk phone played the intercom tone; the display showed "GIFT SHOP." I picked up.

"Yes?"

"Um, Ellen?" said Dee's voice, "Detective—"

"I'm taking the bank deposit," said Kris, pausing in the doorway. "Need me to pick anything up?"

I shook my head, waved goodbye as she headed downstairs, then returned my attention to the phone. "Dee, is he here or did he leave—hic—a message?"

"He's here," she said. Her voice sounded hesitant, as if she was feeling contrite.

Well, and so she should. Trying to give me a heart-attack, or rather getting her brother to do the evil deed.

"Put him in an open alcove. I'll be down in a minute."

"OK. Should I give him some tea?"

I pictured Detective Walters sipping tea. He didn't seem

comfortable.

"Yes, and some scones."

Always entertaining to see what a macho man did with scones.

I hung up, then paused to give myself a silent scold. I was still in a bit of a mood. I swallowed some tea, reminding myself to be kind to Dee (who hadn't meant to annoy me) and to the detective (who could cause me grief if he wanted to).

Should I ask him about the knife?

Daniel Swazo's image returned to me, eyes burning and the knife displayed in his upraised palm, held there by fingertips and thumb. How to phrase a question without arousing Walters's suspicion against myself?

Might not be possible.

I finished the tea in my cup, then went downstairs, taking my phone with me in the hope of being interrupted. I did turn it to silent mode, since I expected no less from my guests.

Dee was at the register, ringing up a sale. I gave her a questioning look and she said "Violet."

Great.

I might as well get used to it. Vi's painting was a part of the tearoom now, a part of my life, and while the reminder was still a bit painful, it was also sweet. And I loved the new décor in the Violet alcove. I slipped through Poppy and Dahlia and stepped into Violet, letting the door drape fall behind me.

"Sorry to keep you waiting—Oh!"

"That's about what I was going to say to you," said Tony Aragón as he rose from the wing chair by the window with a weary smile.

6

"TONY!" I SMILED while my heart did a fluttery dance.

He wore his usual black leather jacket over black shirt and jeans. His hair was slightly mussed; I spotted his motorcycle helmet tucked beside his chair. I had to resist a sudden urge to fling myself into his arms. The alcove was not as private as it seemed.

"Please sit down," I said, leading by example. A pot of tea and two cups sat on the table, along with a small plate of scones. I lifted the cozy from the pot and poured the tea. The warm smell of keemun arose. "I'm glad to see you. I thought it was Detective—hic—Walters again."

"Again?"

"He was here yesterday."

"I thought you were closed on Mondays."

"We are. He came to tell me the autopsy results."

Tony spooned sugar into his cup and stirred it, looking thoughtful. He also looked tired; there were shadows beneath his eyes.

"How's your case going?"

He grimaced as he picked up his cup and drank. "Not great. Got a zillion witnesses, most of them related to each other, all telling different stories."

"I thought it was a gang fight."

"It was. Happened at a wedding."

"Oh, lord!"

"Yeah, it's a cluster...it's a big mess."

I couldn't help smiling. I pushed the scones toward him, taking one myself.

"Well, thank you for stopping by."

"Can't stay long," he said, slathering lemon curd on half a scone. "I just wanted to apologize for not being able to do the movie Thursday."

"We'll find another time. I'm more concerned about Saturday. Do you—hic—think you'll still be able to come?"

He looked at me blankly. "Saturday."

"Tea with your mother and grandmother."

He winced. "Oh—sh—um. I don't know."

"Would it be less stressful if we rescheduled?"

"Not really. Abuela will give me hell. She's looking forward to it big time—getting Mom to fix up one of her dresses."

I was also looking forward to it, but I didn't want to add to his stress by saying so. "Well, you can cancel if you need to. Just call by Saturday morning."

"OK, but I don't plan on canceling. I'll find the time."

I smiled. "I'm glad you found time to come by today."

"I wanted to see you."

He took a bite of scone and gazed at me, dark eyes steady and candid. A tingle moved up my neck.

"Well, I wanted to see—hic—see you, too. I need a reference from you for a reenactor who'd be willing to talk to Willow's tour guests."

"Oh, right." He took out his phone. "Sorry, I meant to get back to you on that."

He gave me a couple of names and numbers to try. I added them to my phone, then took a bite of scone.

"You changed this room," Tony said, nodding toward the portrait of Vi.

"Yes, in her honor. It's Violet now."

"Nice."

"Julio painted that."

Tony looked impressed, and gave the painting a longer glance. "Multi-talented."

"Yes."

He finished the tea in his cup and set it on the table. I reached for the pot, but he shook his head.

"Gotta go. I'll call you when I get time."

"May I ask you one question?" I said.

"Sure."

I sipped my tea, gathering courage. "Would it be possible for you to find out about a piece of evidence?"

He met my gaze. "You mean on a case I'm not working. Yeah, but why don't you just ask Walters?"

"I thought he might misunderstand my curiosity."

Tony's eyes narrowed, then he nodded. "Yeah, OK. He doesn't know you. What evidence do you want to know about?"

"A knife. It was found in Nat's driveway. A folding knife, with a stone-inlaid handle."

"OK. What do you want to know about it?"

"I'm not sure. Just if there's anything unusual about it, I guess."

"I'll check."

"Thank you. Hic."

We both stood, and Tony picked up his helmet. "You should drink a glass of water or something."

"Good idea."

I walked out front with him and watched as he got on his bike and rode away. There was a touch of evening chill in the air, and a breeze blew a small swirl of fallen leaves along the street. The roses in my garden looked tired in the late sunlight. I needed to go out and prune them.

Nat joined me as Tony swung around the corner and out of sight. "Do you mind if I go home, Ellen? It's pretty quiet, and I'd like to start dinner for Manny."

"Of course not. Thanks for coming in. Should I come ov—hic —over after dinner to work on the dress?"

"Absolutely not. You rest up and get over those hiccups. Stay in and read a book."

"Yes, ma'am!"

She gave me a hug, then held me at arms length. "You didn't get much sleep last night, did you?"

I shrugged. "I got some."

"Take a sleeping pill tonight." She opened the door and went in, heading down the hall toward the back. I followed.

"I don't have any."

"I'll get you some."

"No—Nat, you don't have to—"

"It's no trouble. I'll be back in a jiffy."

She paused at the back door and smooched my cheek. "We have plenty of time to finish the dress. Come over on Sunday, and don't worry about it before then."

"All right."

I watched her go, then headed for the kitchen. Dee came out of the pantry as I entered the side hallway.

"Thanks for setting up the tea and scones for Violet," I told her, smiling. "You can clear when you get a minute."

"I just did."

"Excellent."

In the kitchen I found Julio wiping down the counters. "How big a pumpkin do you want?" I asked.

"Why don't I just pick it up myself?"

"In that case, feel free to go home all of—" I checked my watch. "—fifteen minutes early."

"Thanks, boss."

"You're—hic—welcome."

He gave me a wry look, then took off his apron and hat, grabbed his coat, and left. I drifted back to the main hallway. The day was ending; only one party remained in the main parlor. Feeling restless and a little sad, I opened the door of the dining parlor and stepped in.

Soft, indirect light through the sheers set the room gently aglow in twilight, with deep shadows in the corners away from the window presaging the night. By Halloween, the sun would be down at this hour, and candlelight would give this room a cozy glow.

Perhaps I should set out candles for Willow's October tea tours. Just a couple, for atmosphere. We could light them right before the guests arrived, and maybe the reenactor could talk about Captain Dusenberry by candlelight, and then we'd turn on the chandelier.

As if in answer to my thoughts, the chandelier came on. I blinked at the sudden brilliance, and glanced toward the light switch by the door. No one there.

"Thank you, Captain," I said softly. "I'm glad you approve."

I hoped he approved. Maybe I was making up reasons for his turning the lights on. Maybe it was all my imagination and could be explained by old wiring.

But it had been a while since I'd believed that. The captain's activities had gone on long enough, and occurred at enough significant moments, that I was convinced he was really here. He'd turned on the stereo, playing specific pieces of music. He'd played the piano in the parlor, which could not be attributed to wiring.

My invisible roommate.

I looked at the chandelier, half expecting to see a single crystal swaying, but it was still.

My phone rang. I went into the hall to answer it, which in a way made no sense, as I was leaving a private room. But it was the captain's room, and I didn't want to disturb him with my phone call.

"Don't start dinner," Gina said after my greeting. "I'm coming over."

"I don't—hic—have a TV, remember."

"I'm not bringing the movie. I *am* bringing a pizza. Do you have wine?"

"Yes."

"Perfecto. See you in a few."

I checked the time: 6:01. Even as I glanced toward the front door, I heard the sound of the bells jingle, and saw Dee locking up. She turned off the lights in the gift shop and parlor, and came toward me, untying her apron.

"Thanks, Dee. See you tomorrow."

"Sorry about the hiccup thing."

"It's all right."

I tried to suppress a hiccup, but she noticed; she gave me a rueful glance before stepping into the pantry to hang up her apron. I moved to lock the back door and saw Nat coming toward it, so I opened it instead.

"Here you are," she said, handing me a small blue and white box. "Half of one is plenty."

"Thanks, Nat. Give my love to Manny."

"I will."

I locked the back door, waving at Dee and Mick who were leaving through the kitchen's separate door. I watched to make sure they locked it, then headed upstairs.

Pizza night merited a change of clothes. I took off my dress and pulled on my sweats, then took a bottle of Malbec out of my small wine cellar and opened it to let it breathe. Gina and I had been exploring Malbecs recently; there were quite a few good ones coming out of Argentina. It took a small exercise of willpower to refrain from pouring myself a glass immediately.

Instead, I followed Tony's advice and drank a glass of water. No noticeable impact on the hiccups, but I'm sure it was good for me.

My phone, which I'd left on a side table, began humming and vibrating itself toward the edge. I grabbed it and saw Gina's number, so I answered irreverently: "Wisteria Sushi, what's your favorite fish?"

"Anchovies. Come down and let me in, I'm going to have my hands full."

I hurried downstairs and unlocked the back door. Gina's moon-shaped face glowed with a grin as she balanced a pizza box and two large carryout bags. She must have come straight after work, because she had on a bright red linen skirt and jacket over a cream silk blouse, one of the outfits she called her ad exec uniforms.

"Let's eat this while it's hot. Dining parlor?"

"The wine's upstairs," I said, relieving her of the pizza. The smell of hot garlic taunted me.

"Fair enough."

We climbed up and Gina headed for the sitting area by the front window. I turned on the chandelier, then fetched the wine, glasses, and a couple of plates from my suite.

"Put this in your freezer," Gina said, handing me a package of ice cream from one of the bags.

"Mint chocolate ch-hic?"

"I couldn't find peppermint. Dinner first, though."

I put away the ice cream and returned to see Gina arranging containers of salad and garlic bread on the coffee table.

"Who else is coming?" I asked, sitting down and helping myself to a slice of pizza.

She tilted her head to smirk at me. "Hah, hah."

I took a bite: green chile, mushroom, and Canadian bacon. "Mm. My favorite."

"Only the best for my BFF. Pass the wine."

"What's in there?" I asked, pointing to a large plastic storage container as I handed her the bottle.

"Lasagna from the other night. That goes in the freezer too."

"It's full of ice cream."

"Gelato, actually. Your freezer isn't that tiny."

"Want to bet? Hic."

"You can put it downstairs, then."

"I'm sure Julio will enjoy it."

Gina poured generous glasses for both of us, then raised hers in a toast. "To hell with the hiccups."

"I'll drink to that."

We ate and drank in silence for a few minutes, then Gina put another slice of pizza on her plate and leaned toward me.

"So tell me."

"About what?"

"Finding your latest body."

"He's not *my* body. And I thought I already told you."

"Sketchily. I want all the details."

I took a swallow of wine, then started at the beginning. Gina listened intently, nodding now and then. She frowned when I described Detective Walters's visit to the tearoom during my meltdown, and again when I told her about my dream visit from Daniel Swazo.

"Girlfriend, you need to see a therapist."

"I went and talked to that counselor from the Hospice Center today. Loren Ja—hic—Jackson."

"Did that help?"

"Yes." I nodded, then took another piece of pizza. "He's very nice. He really listens."

"Really cute, too, if I remember right."

"Did I say that?"

"Didn't you?"

I frowned, doubting I had said any such thing to Gina. "Well, anyway, he helped me realize that the knife in my dream was the same one the cops f—hic—found in Nat's driveway. I asked Tony to check if there was anything unusual about it."

"How come Tony isn't investigating this?"

"He's on another case, a nasty one."

"Oh."

Gina finished a slice of pizza, looked speculatively at the rest of the pie and at the garlic bread, then helped herself to a virtuous serving of salad. I followed suit, actually glad to have the greens.

"Thank you for bringing this," I said.

"Well, I've been worried about you."

"I'm all—hic—right."

"Uh-huh."

I refilled our wine glasses. "How's your week going?"

"Busy. Everybody's getting their holiday ads in."

"This early?"

"Be glad you're not already seeing them. It won't be long."

"Ugh. Sorry, no offense."

"None taken. Truth be told, I think they should ban Christmas ads until after Thanksgiving. Don't tell my boss I said that."

"Or at least until after Halloween."

"Hm." Gina took a piece of garlic bread and used it to push

the last of her salad onto her fork. "So one question, and then I'll take off my ad hat. Have you got your Christmas ads planned?"

"It's September! I don't even have Halloween done!"

"Christmas is more important."

"Not in this house," I muttered.

"I know you always loved Halloween, but—"

"I love *all* holidays!"

"Dressing up for Halloween was always your favorite." She picked up her wineglass and gestured with it. "Remember the mermaid costume? And in mid-school, when you decided to go as La Llorona? Scared half the little kids to death."

"I like Christmas too!" I said defensively.

"Good, because you should get your ads done and in by the end of the month, or all the best slots will be taken."

I closed my eyes, inhaled deeply, and hiccuped. "I'd rather not talk about work, if you don't mind," I said with dignity.

"OK. Let's talk about something else. Other than being on a nasty case, how's your boyfriend?"

"He's not my—hic—boyfriend." I picked up a piece of garlic bread.

"When's the last time you saw him?"

"This afternoon, as a matter of fact."

"Is he going to the wedding?"

"I haven't asked him."

"Why not?"

I took a large bite of garlic bread, preventing my answering immediately. Tony might be off weddings right at the moment, considering the case he was working on. I really wanted to wait until after our tea with his family before deciding.

"Ask him," Gina crooned, reaching for the wine bottle. "You know you want to."

"He might think I'm being too pushy. We haven't even been on a real date."

She poured the last of the wine into our glasses. "I thought you went to the opera."

"That was a group party. Doesn't count, and besides he

ended up working."

"And the movies."

"Not yet. We still haven't found the right time."

"Tsk. If you're not careful, you're going to be an old maid."

"Gina! Nobody says 'old maid' anymore."

"Nonna Fiorello does. Says it to me every chance she gets."

I took a swallow of wine. "I love Nonna Fiorello, but I'm glad she's not—hic—my grandmother. She would drive me nuts."

"Eh. It's how we know she loves us. Here's to Nonna Fiorello."

Gina drained her glass. I had too much wine left to do the same, but I took a big swig. I was beginning to feel the effects of the alcohol. I cupped the bowl of my glass in my palms and swirled the wine around.

"Have you brought her to the tearoom?" I asked.

"Nonna? No. Should I?"

"Would she like it?"

Gina took a bite of garlic bread and chewed, looking thoughtful. "Yeah, she probably would. You're right, I should bring her."

"Maybe I'll do a 'bring your grandmother to tea' special," I mused.

"It's called Mother's Day."

"Don't they have a Grandmother's Day, too? When is that?"

"How should I know?"

"You're the ad person. Don't you guys kee—hic—keep track of all that stuff?"

"Heck, we make up a lot of it." She tipped up her wineglass and collected a last ruby-colored drop. "Grandmother's Day. Sheesh."

"You sound like you don't like your job."

"I *love* my job. I just sometimes don't like my profession."

I nodded. That sounded profound, but maybe it was the influence of the wine.

"OK," Gina said, standing and flipping the pizza box closed. "Time for gelato."

"Shouldn't we wait a bit? I'm—hic—kind of full."

"Full is good. We want your diaphragm to be stretched out. Then we hit it with the gelato, and presto!"

Sighing, I helped collect our plates and the leftovers. The pizza box was twice the width of my mini-fridge, so I stacked the slices of pizza on a plate with paper towels between them. The salad went into my fridge as well; the garlic bread and the lasagna went downstairs. By the time I came back, Gina was dishing up gelato in my kitchenette. She handed me a heaping bowl.

"That's too much!"

"Eat it fast."

I took a bite. "Mmm. Pretty good." I looked at the container.

"New brand. Eat, eat."

I ate, taking time to let the bits of dark chocolate dissolve on my tongue. Gina carried her bowl to the two chairs I had by the chimney, and I joined her.

"So, my day was full of Christmas fol-de-rol," she said. "We're working on an ad for my favorite used car dealership."

"Oh, no—Zyler?"

She glared at me. "Your mouth should be full."

I hastily took another bite. I made it a small one, because my stomach was starting to feel the pressure.

"Yes, Zyler. He comes in and wants an ad with a car in a Santa hat and white beard and mustache. Not a drawing, mind—but a photo. Eat."

I took another tiny bite. Gina frowned, so I took bigger one.

"I tell him it's a stupid idea," she went on. "Actually, that's what I'm thinking, but what I tell him is that unless it's a goatee, the beard will drag on the ground and give the wrong impression."

She pointed her spoon at me. I ate another bite of gelato. My throat was getting cold.

"Turns out he's got a buddy who's already built the Santa hat. Zyler shows me a picture of it on his phone. It looks like a giant red traffic cone."

I couldn't help laughing. Then I hiccuped.

"More gelato," Gina ordered. "So he's got his heart set on this traffic cone. I can't talk him out of it. We have a photo shoot on Friday. It's going to be a disaster."

"Oh, Gina. I'm so sorry."

"Eat! It's his money, if he wants to spend it that way, I can't stop him."

I didn't dare answer for fear of being ordered to consume more gelato. I'd reached my limit. The cold was spreading down my chest.

"You've still got half a bowl," Gina said.

I shook my head, drew a breath, and went into a fit of coughing, punctuated with hiccups. Cough-hic. Cough-hic. It was painful.

I put my bowl down and stood, trying to get control of my breathing. Pressed both hands against my chest, still cough-hiccing.

"Dang," Gina commented.

It took me another minute to be able to draw breath without coughing. I bent down, picked up my bowl, and hiccuped. I felt unwell.

"Wow, I've never had that happen," Gina said.

"Let's go for a—hic—walk."

She ate the last bite of her (much smaller) serving of gelato, stood, and took my bowl, putting it with hers in the sink. I fetched my keys and my phone, and we went downstairs. I wanted to keep moving, to appease my overtaxed digestive system.

We went out the back door and I locked it behind us. The evening was mild, with just enough breeze to stimulate the circulation and stir up the aroma of dry leaves on fading grass. I turned north at the end of the drive, because there were more bushes that way, though I hoped I would not need to be sick behind one of them.

"I'm sorry," Gina said, keeping pace with me. "It really does work."

"It's all right. These aren't your av—hic—average hiccups."

"I guess not."

We reached Federal place, an oval street that I always thought of as a race track that surrounded the main post office and the old Federal Building. I decided a lap would do me good, and lengthened my stride a bit.

"Now there's an old building for you," Gina said, looking at the Federal Building. "I wonder if it has any ghosts."

"Ask Willow."

"Is it older than the tearoom?"

"I don't think so. I know that it was par—hic—partially built when the Civil War began, so it sat unfinished for a few years. My house is antebellum."

"That word always makes me think of Scarlett O'Hara."

The Federal Building was kind of pretty, in a blocky stone way. Much nicer than the neighboring post office, which was circa 1960s. We paused to admire the statue of Kit Carson at the south side, then headed back toward my house.

"You want to walk around the Plaza?" Gina asked.

"Not tonight. Think I'm going to turn in early. I didn't sl—hic —sleep very well last night."

"What you need is a good lay."

I laughed. "Gina!"

"I'm serious. Take your mind off it, relieve your tension. Call Tony. Or that cute counselor. Somebody."

"I'll keep it in mind."

To be honest, I hadn't had a good lay in quite a while. I'd been too busy in the last couple of years, and too grief-stricken, and too lacking in prospects.

She might very well be right, but for me it wasn't as simple as making a phone call. Not right now. I was still busy; still—or again—grieving.

We reached my driveway and walked up it. Gina's red Camaro sat next to my much more sedate Camry. I opened the door, and Gina hung back.

"If you're going to bed, I'll head home. Sleep better tonight."

"Thanks. And thanks for the pizza. And the gelato. I'll—hic—try it again tomorrow."

"It always works the first time for me," she said, shaking her head.

"Oh, well. You never know."

I hugged her, then went inside and watched her get into her car and drive away. The walk had settled my too-large meal, but I wasn't quite ready for bed. I tidied up the sitting area and my suite, then took a long, hot, shower.

The blue package Nat had given me lay on my bed. Sleeping pills. I'd never needed them in my life, but this was an extraordinary circumstance. I pulled out the bottle and shook a blue pill into my palm. Remembering Nat's parting words, I broke it in half and washed one piece down with half a glass of water.

I crawled under the covers and snuggled into my pillows with my current novel, a fluffy tale about a cat in outer space. When the words started dancing on the page, I set the book aside and turned out the light.

Pounding on my door woke me. I turned over, peering at my clock. Something must have been wrong with it, because it read 9:15.

"Ellen?" Kris called through the door of my suite. "Are you all right?"

Muttering a curse, I dragged myself out of bed and stumbled to my closet. Groggy. I pulled on my robe and shuffled to the door, unlocking it and opening it a crack. I saw a sliver of Kris: dark purple dress, dark hair, dark lips, and one eye outlined meticulously in kohl.

"Oh, good," she said. "I was getting worried!"

"Sorry," I mumbled. "Took a slee—hic—py pill."

"OK. Well, Willow's on the phone. I'll tell her you'll call her back."

"'Kay. Be right out."

It took me rather longer than I expected to pull myself together. I wondered if Nat had mistakenly bought pills intended for a horse. I distinctly remembered her saying half a pill, and that was what I had taken, and it was too much. I was still half asleep.

I managed to dress myself in a skirt and a light sweater. No buttons. I needed to wake up more before attempting makeup.

Walking carefully, I crossed the hall to my office. A tea tray sat on the credenza in Kris's, and I silently blessed Kris or whoever had thought of it as I poured myself a cup. I drank it at my desk, gazing stupidly at a pile of message slips.

Kris stepped in, looking warily at me. "Everything OK?"

"Yeah, I just—hic—well..."

I put my head in my hands. Took a deep breath, then looked at Kris and started again. "I'm all right. Sorry I overslept."

"No problem. Just worried about you."

"Too much sleep aid, that's all."

She nodded, then stepped forward to hand me another lavender slip. "Here's Willow's message."

"Thanks."

The message was about the reenactor, of course. The first of Willow's tea tours was less than two weeks away. I needed to nail that down.

Phone. I needed my cell phone—that was where I had put the numbers Tony gave me. I fetched it from my suite, and noticed that I had a new text from Tony.

Knife had meth residue

Meth! Holy crap!

I could not believe that Daniel Swazo had been a meth addict. He was so polite, so quiet, so nice...

Actually, I didn't know him at all. Those were my impressions, but impressions could be mistaken. I hadn't even talked with him. I'd only seen him once...alive.

I couldn't deal with the murder right now. I sent Tony a quick text of thanks, looked up the reenactors' numbers and wrote them on the message from Willow, then sat trying to organize my thoughts about what to say when I called them.

A knock made me look up. Julio stood in the doorway, holding a steaming mug and a small plate.

"Heard you might need a little help waking up," he said.

"Oh—uh—"

"This is my Colombian blend." He set the mug in front of me, along with a small pitcher of cream. Just the aroma was caffeinated enough to make me open my eyes wider.

"And this is something I'd like you to try. It's a possible new item for October."

The plate he set before me held three small, round, lumpy-looking, not-quite-cookie things.

"What are they?"

"Pumpkin fritters."

I put a dollop of cream in the coffee and took a swig. The warmth flowed down my chest and lit a gentle glow in my stomach. One more swallow, then I picked up one of the fritters.

It was lighter than I expected, and crunchier, and almost immediately melted in my mouth. It was slightly sweet, but with the natural sweetness of the pumpkin itself. The flavor was wonderful, with just a hint of buttery saltiness.

"Mmmm. Oh, Julio." I took another bite. "That's fantastic!"

He smiled. "You like?"

"Mm." I finished the first fritter and picked up another. "Are they ha—hic—hard to make?"

"Not really. They won't be. I had to fiddle with the proportions a bit, but I think I've got it down now."

"It's great. Much better than pumpkin pie."

"Well, I hope so. I wanted to do something different."

"They're perfect. You're brilliant."

"Only thing is, they don't keep. I tried storing some overnight and they got soft."

I eyed the other two fritters on my plate. "I don't think that will be a problem."

He smiled. "Glad you like them. I'll talk to Kris about the

price."

"Good work." I drank some more coffee. "And thank you. This is breakfast. I'm—hic—sure you knew that."

He tossed a grin over his shoulder as he headed into Kris's office. I raised the mug to him, then used its contents to wash down the fritters.

I felt a lot better. Still a little groggy, but the food and coffee helped.

Reenactors. I took out a notepad and organized my thoughts, then called the first number. Got voicemail, left a message, called the second and had better luck. Yes, he might be available; yes, he might be interested in portraying, if not Captain Dusenberry himself, then a soldier from his era. I made a tentative arrangement for him to come to the tearoom the next day to meet with me and Willow, then called Willow to confirm.

"Ah, Ellen," she answered. "It's good to hear your voice. How are you feeling?"

"A little sluggish today. I took—hic—too much sleep aid last night."

"Oh? Well, I hope you got a good night's sleep, at least."

We finalized the meeting plans. I called the reenactor back to verify. All set.

With that task off my mind, I was able to deal with most of the other messages. I set the one from Bennett Cole aside—that was more a personal project—and had just returned the last of the business calls when Nat came in.

She had on a wine-colored dress with a pretty, cashmere scarf in autumn colors. She wished me a good morning, to which I responded with a skeptical glance.

"Half a pill?"

"Manny always takes a half. I take less; usually only a quarter."

"I wish you had to—hic—told me that."

"Oh, dear—I'm sorry. Did you oversleep?"

"Kris had to roust me."

I could tell she was smothering a laugh. Her eyes had the

same smile lines they got when she was teasing Manny. "Well, I'm sure you must have needed the rest."

As punishment, I sent her downstairs with my breakfast plate and Julio's coffee mug. Feeling closer to reasonably awake, I went across the hall to put on makeup, change my ponytail for a more elegant coiffure, and swap my sweater for a silk blouse.

The day went fairly smoothly. I ate leftover salad for lunch, heard back from the first reenactor (October was a busy month for him, but he was willing to back up the other guy), and continued to hiccup. My staff offered no more cures, for which I was privately grateful.

That night I stayed home, ate pizza, read a book, and gave the gelato another try. I didn't overeat, but I did have a pretty generous bowl of mint chocolate chip, and I tried to eat it pretty fast. I did not freeze my chest again, or go into a coughing fit. Nor did I get rid of the hiccups, but at least there was chocolate.

I surfed the web for hiccup information. Many of the home remedies that my dear friends and family had inflicted on me popped up, along with a few others that I hoped no one would suggest. Under medical treatment, I found a rather alarming list of sedatives and even anti-psychotics that were sometimes prescribed for hiccup sufferers. I did *not* want to go that route. By contrast, the sleeping pills didn't look so bad.

I eyed the bottle on my nightstand when I came to bed. Half a pill was definitely too much. Would a quarter still be too much? I could probably break a pill into eighths, but what if that wasn't enough and I couldn't get to sleep? I decided to try a quarter and set my alarm just in case.

As I lay staring up at the brocade canopy of my bed, waiting for the pill to take effect, I thought through the day's unfinished business. I should make a few notes for the meeting with Willow and the reenactor tomorrow. I still needed to talk to Bennett Cole about the Colt Navy revolvers.

My thoughts wandered off through other parts of the day, and ended up walking with Gina through nighttime Santa Fe. We walked around the Federal Building on the race track, then uphill toward Fort Marcy Park, where Zozobra was burned every year as part of Fiesta. One of my favorite memories from childhood: picnicking on a blanket in the park, waiting for it to get dark so the giant paper puppet could be burned. Old Man Gloom—burn him, and all your troubles with him. No more troubles for a year.

The park was dark now, and empty. Zozobra stood alone on his platform, unmoving, silent. Resigned to his fate.

I looked for the Fire Dancer but didn't see him. He was the one who set Zozobra on fire. We needed to do that—to get rid of the gloom. I started up the steps toward the platform, but I didn't know the dance, and I didn't have any torches. I kept looking, searching for help, for the right tools.

At the top of the steps a figure stood waiting for me, silhouetted against the ghostly white of Zozobra's long robe. Not the Fire Dancer, because it didn't have the tall headdress with the red feathers dancing at the ends of long wires like flames in the night.

It was just a man. He raised his hand in a too-familiar gesture.

It was Daniel Swazo, holding his folded knife for me to see.

I nodded, trying to show him I understood. The knife was important, yes. I'd asked about it. There was meth on it.

Swazo looked angry, and opened his mouth. Zozobra's roar came out of it, and Swazo's eyes lit up neon green and he shook his head from side to side, like Zozobra did when the Fire Dancer taunted him.

Then he burst into flames.

7

I SAT UP with a muffled cry of alarm, then subsided into tears and hiccups. After a minute I turned on the light on my nightstand. I drank the water in my bedside glass. Stumbled out of bed and into my robe, turning lights on every time I got near a switch.

Dammit, dammit, dammit. Was Swazo trying to communicate, or was it just my over-stressed mind trying to decompress?

I needed a drink. The most convenient option was port, from a bottle I kept for an occasional late-night glass. I poured it generously and walked out into the hallway, taking a big swallow as I headed for the front window.

The sheers were drawn over it, framed by the heavier drapes. I stood looking through them at the street lights and other lights outside—soft, glowing blobs.

Why? Why was I dreaming about Swazo?

I needed to talk to someone.

My first thought was Loren Jackson. He'd said to call anytime, but I suspected yuck-o-clock in the morning was not what he'd meant.

I didn't want to bother Gina, or Nat. I decided to compose an email to Willow, which I wouldn't really send. I just needed to sort through my thoughts.

I turned on the overhead light in my office, a Tiffany-style stained-glass bowl that cast soft, jewel-toned light through the room. For good measure I turned on the standing lamp by my chaise longue as well. Then I sat at my desk and brought up my email software. Ignoring the waiting messages—work-related, mostly—I opened a new message, typed Willow's name at the top, then spilled my worries onto the screen.

You are the ghost expert. Maybe you can help me. I just
had a nightmare. Daniel Swazo is haunting my dreams,
and this time he pulled a Zozobra and went up in flames.

This is the second time I've dreamed about Daniel Swazo.
I'm wondering if these are messages from him, if he's
trying to tell me something. He keeps showing me his
knife, a knife that he made, that was found in Nat's
driveway where he died. I asked Detective Aragón to
check it and he said the knife had meth residue on it. I
don't think Swazo was doing meth, but I might be wrong.

Or is he trying to warn me about meth? I don't have
anything to do with it.

I paused, wondering if anyone I knew was involved with
meth. A dreadful thought! I trusted everyone on my staff, but
even good people can do terrible things if they have an addiction.

The most obvious candidates for any dubious scenario were
Kris and Ramon, the two with Goth connections. Not that Goth
and meth were automatically related, but those two were the
only members of my staff who had committed anything
resembling crimes, that I knew of. Minor transgressions, granted.
Ramon had trespassed (on my property) and Kris had talked
back to the police and been arrested for it. Bottom line: they were
both risk-takers. Either of them might get into trouble without
intending to.

I hiccuped, then took another swallow of port. Probably I
was thinking too hard. I went back to my pretend email.

I keep thinking Swazo is trying to tell me something. If it
isn't meth, then it's something else about the knife, but
what? I don't understand.

Back to that. What did it mean?

Maybe it didn't mean anything. Maybe I was obsessing on
knives because of Victor Solano's murder at the Opera. Maybe I
was just tired and stressed. I moved to close the email, but my

hand did what it was used to and hit "send."

"Shit!"

Belatedly I hit "cancel," but the message had already gone out.

I grabbed my port glass and started pacing.

Great. Just great. Now Willow would think I was nuts. And I'd told her things about the investigation that she shouldn't know. I'd violated Tony's confidence. Damn, damn, damn.

I'd just have to write another email to Willow telling her to ignore the first one. I drank the rest of my port and returned to my desk, intending to do that, but there was a new message.

From Willow.

I glanced at the time on the screen: 2:56. Willow was a night-owl, apparently.

Gritting my teeth, I opened her message, already composing an apology.

Ellen -

I'm glad you wrote. I sensed a spirit near you the last time we met, and I don't doubt that it was Daniel Swazo. It's very likely that he is trying to communicate with you. Don't let that worry you—I'm positive that he's not a harmful spirit. He's not going to hurt you or deliberately frighten you. As you deduced, he's just trying to tell you something that he thinks is important.

When a spirit has an urgent message like this, he or she cannot cross over properly, and remains stuck between planes. I'm happy to help in any way I can, so that Daniel can be at peace and you can relax.

Can you tell me more about your dreams?

- Willow

Whoa. She sensed Swazo's spirit near me?

I swallowed, wishing I had more port. Closing my eyes, I

took a deep breath.

I was kind of at a crossroads here. Either I bought into Willow's—whatever it was, her view of the world—or I called it bull and stuck to what I could see and touch.

Willow was nice but she'd always made me just a little uncomfortable. I'd never pinpointed the reason before, but now I realized it was because she, not I, was Captain Dusenberry's number one fan. Heck, she'd come by the tearoom before it first opened to ask to see his study. She was utterly convinced that he was real, that he was present in this house, more than a hundred and fifty years after his death.

And I, though I was increasingly convinced, still had my doubts. Self-doubt, more than anything else. Was I lying to myself? Was it wishful thinking to believe that I had an invisible roommate?

Strains of violin music floated up from downstairs; the stereo that played music through the tearoom during business hours had come on. I stiffened, listening until I recognized the piece. Mozart. Of course.

I sighed. Who was I to say that only the tangible was real?

Biting my lip, I opened a reply to Willow's email. I described both dreams to her, in as much detail as I could remember. Then I asked her not to mention the knife to anyone, as it was part of the Swazo murder investigation.

I sent the message off, picked up my port glass, and carried it back to my suite. It took an effort to decide that more port would actually be a bad idea. Instead I poured myself a glass of water and went back to my desk.

No answer yet from Willow. I leaned back in my chair, thinking of Zozobra.

I'd missed Fiesta this year. Too busy with the tearoom. Actually, I hadn't been to Zozobra for several years. It was just too crowded lately, and the show had become more and more elaborate.

I missed the simpler, more straightforward event I remembered from years ago. Just the Fire Dancer, and the little

Glooms (Cub Scouts in sheets), and a few extra folks mostly there to keep everyone safe. And Zozobra's loud, amplified moaning, and his marionette arms flailing as he wagged his head from side to side. That was all he could do: shake his head and flail his arms and yell, but it had always been exciting enough.

Sometimes I felt like that was all I could do, too. Shake my head, flail, yell.

And then, after Zozobra was finally ablaze, fireworks filled the air and everyone cheered. The fireworks continued, and finally the giant would collapse into a smoldering heap on the platform. More cheering, then the fireworks would end, and the stadium lights would come on, and everyone would drift away home or to the hundreds of parties going on all over town. Fiesta.

I hiccuped. My email software pinged with a new message from Willow.

Ellen -

I believe you're right that Daniel wants you to know something about the knife. Since it's a piece of evidence, I'm assuming no way for us to look at it. Is there any other information about it?

- Willow

I wrote a quick answer, telling her about the knives I'd seen on Daniel Swazo's table at the flea market, describing his knife in detail—which I could do with perfect confidence, its image having been burned into my brain by now—and promising to ask Tony if there was any more information. I doubted there would be, but I'd ask.

I was yawning by now, so I added a thank-you to Willow for listening, then sent the message off and went back to bed.

I woke to the sound of rain on the metal roof. A glance at my clock told me I had anticipated the alarm by a few minutes. I slid out of bed and put the kettle on, and managed to be presentable by the time the smell of baking scones had wafted up the stairwell.

I pushed aside the sheers on the front window, and saw gray sky to the horizon and a slow, gentle rain falling. A soaking rain, not a cloudburst. If we were lucky, it would go on all day.

Feeling a need for some solid human company, I went down to say hello to Julio. He had the salsa music on low and was dancing from sink to cutting board to work table. His chef's pants and hat were out of a fabric covered in autumn leaves: red, orange, and yellow on a black background.

"You must have a really big closet," I remarked.

He glanced up at me, flashing a grin. "Tell you a secret. Andre and I trade. We wear the same size, except he's taller."

I glanced at his feet. The pants did bag there a bit, but not badly.

"So you both have a double—hic—wardrobe. Sweet."

"Well, there are a few patterns he won't wear. He doesn't like the hibiscus flowers."

"Too girly?"

Julio shrugged. "He's not flashy."

I smiled. I wouldn't have called Julio flashy, either—at least, not when I first met him. He definitely had a serious streak. It didn't keep him from being willing to play, though, much to my occasional delight.

"You need breakfast?" he asked.

"I don't know...are you making pumpkin fritters?"

"Not today."

"Then I'll fix myself something. Thanks, though."

I went to the butler's pantry and made a pot of tea. Dee came in and smiled as she put on her apron.

"Fires today?" she asked.

"Sure," I said. "It's chilly."

When my tea was ready, I carried it upstairs. Kris wasn't there yet, so I breakfasted in secret on cold pizza and tea before going to my desk.

No new email, but Willow's last message reminded me that I needed to ask Tony about the knife. I got my phone, intending to text him, then decided email would be better. He might think a text needed immediate attention, and I didn't want my question to take him away from his case.

To be honest, I was little embarrassed to be bothering him about the knife again. He'd already gone out of his way to check it for me. But I'd promised Willow I'd ask, so I opened an email.

Tony -

Was there anything else in the report about the knife? Anything at all? I'm having dreams about Daniel Swazo. Trying to make them stop.

Thanks,

- Ellen

I sat staring at it before sending it off. Would he think I was stupid? Annoying? Crazy? Should I just erase it and start over?

Not that again. Very deliberately, I hit "send."

If Tony thought I was a nut case, so be it. I lived in a haunted house. Very gently haunted, by a pretty nice ghost, all things considered. But still.

I pulled up our reservations schedule to check how busy we'd be. Not very; late September was a slow time. Fiesta was over, as were the opera season and the big Markets. A lot of locals were off at the State Fair in Albuquerque. Most of the tourists had left, and things would be slower until December, when the skiing and holiday seasons would bring more visitors.

That and the rain made for a quiet day. I had the meeting with Willow and the reenactor in the early afternoon, but that was about it. I set to work on clearing up the tasks I'd set aside for "later."

Just before noon I went downstairs for another pot of tea, and found Iz polishing spoons in the pantry. She looked up and smiled as I put on the kettle. I hiccuped.

"Iz, may I ask your opinion? Do you think Daniel Swazo might have been a drug addict?"

"Daniel? No. He was a good person. *He* didn't mess with that stuff."

"You think maybe someone he knew did?"

She sniffed and went back to rubbing a spoon. "His brother isn't so good. Makes their mom crazy."

"His brother?"

"Older brother. Tomas."

"He's—hic—into drugs?"

"I don't know about that. He just gets into trouble, you know?"

"I see."

The kettle boiled, and I set my tea to steeping. "Did Daniel have any enemies, that you know of?"

Iz shook her head firmly. "Daniel was a good guy."

I thought about that. Maybe no one had wanted to kill Daniel, but someone had certainly beaten him severely.

Becoming aware that my gaze was resting on a canister of oolong, I remembered that I needed leaf tea upstairs. I took out a plastic bag and took down the Darjeeling.

"But was anybody on his case?" I asked gently as I scooped tea leaves into the bag. "You know, even g—hic—good guys get bullied sometimes."

Iz tilted her head, thinking, then shook it. "Nobody I know about."

"Well, thank you."

She nodded and picked up another spoon. I checked the timer, then went to make a quick pass through the tearoom.

Three parties, all quietly enjoying tea in the main parlor. Nat was in the gift shop, puttering with the bags and wrappings. She brightened as I came in. "Hello, dear! Are you feeling any better?"

"Some. Had a dr—hic—dream about Swazo last night."

"Another one?"

"This time he turned into Zozobra."

Nat put her arm around my shoulders. "Honey, you need to go up to 10 K Waves. Why don't you take the afternoon off?"

"It's raining."

"So get a massage. Sit in the sauna."

"I'll think about it."

Usually a reservation was necessary for a massage at Ten Thousand Waves, but on a slow day like today, they might have openings. I wasn't quite in the mood, though. Imagining myself hiccuping my way through a massage wasn't a tranquil thought.

Lounging on my chaise with a book was a much more appealing image. I promised myself an hour at the end of the afternoon.

Meanwhile, I should try to make myself useful. I collected my tea—both brewed and leaf—and went back upstairs. Took the leaf tea across to my suite, poked my head into Kris's office and saw that she was on the phone, and went to my desk where I sent her a message offering to take the bank deposit after my meeting.

A walk in the rain would do me good, and the bank was just under a mile away. I had a nice, big umbrella and a warm wool coat.

My cell phone rang. I grabbed it, hoping the call was from Tony, but the caller ID showed 'Hospice Center'."

Swallowing disappointment, I answered. "Hello?"

"Hi, Ellen, it's Loren." His voice was warm, and made me think of sitting on the comfortable couch at the Hospice Center. "Just thought I'd follow up on our conversation. Have you been sleeping better?"

"Oh, well—hic—sort of."

"Still hiccuping? Have you called your doctor?"

"Not yet."

"Might be good to make an appointment."

"You're probably right."

There was a pause. I knew he meant well, and I appreciated his kindness, but I couldn't find anything to say.

"I've been thinking about you," he said. "Would you like to talk again? My schedule's pretty free tomorrow."

"Next week would be better. Fridays are pretty busy here."

Not that it looked like this Friday would be. I closed the reservation screen on my computer.

"How about Tuesday again?" Loren said. "Or Monday—you're closed that day, right?"

"Right. Yes. Monday would be good."

"How about eleven o'clock?"

I checked my calendar. Wide open on Monday.

"That's fine," I said, making a note.

"Great. See you then. Have a good weekend, Ellen."

"Thanks. You, too."

I hung up, and set the phone aside, frowning. Why had I been so uncomfortable? Loren was nice. Our talk had done me good.

For lunch, I had leftover salad, and tarnished this virtuous act with one piece of garlic bread on the side. By then, it was time to meet Willow and the reenactor. I tidied my suite and myself, then went downstairs.

The tearoom was cozy: soft music, a few voices of patrons in quiet conversation, a hint of aromatic piñon in the air from the fireplaces. Willow was waiting in one of the chairs by the entrance, her black jacket over a teal sweater setting off her pale hair, a silver heishi necklace spilling like a waterfall down her chest. As I went to greet her, the bells on the front door jingled.

A man—stocky, bearded, with wary eyes—stepped in and closed the door gently behind him. In khaki trousers and a black-and-red plaid wool coat, he did not look like he was here for tea, so I assumed he was the reenactor.

"Mr. Quentin?"

"That's right," he said, nodding. "You Ms. Rosings?"

"Yes, and this is Willow Lane," I said as Willow rose from her chair. "She's the owner of Spirit Tours of Santa Fe. Shall we—hic—go back?"

As I led them down the hall to the dining parlor, I couldn't help thinking that Mr. Quentin was rather older, and rather heavier, than I imagined the typical Civil War Soldier to have been. That was neither here nor there, though. If he knew his subject, then he was the right man for the job.

"Here's the dining parlor," I said, showing them in. The table was set for a party of five; there must be a reservation later in the day.

"This was Dusenberry's office, correct?" he said.

"His study, yes. You're familiar with Captain Dusenberry?"

He nodded, surveying the room with a keen eye. "In a manner of speaking. I've done an impression of him several times. Quartermasters aren't called for very much, but I like to mix things up a little."

Not quite sure I understood that, I went on. "Willow will be bringing tour groups here in October, to finish their tours with a light tea. We'd like you to be he—hic—here to talk about the Captain."

"Do you want a first person impression, or just a talk?"

"I'm not quite sure what you mean."

"First person is when I portray the individual. I dress like him, speak like him, converse as if I were him. I become him, in a sense."

"Oh! Well, I was thinking of having you in uniform..." I looked to Willow.

"A talk would be best, I think," she said. "We'll be discussing his death, and that might be a little awkward if you're doing an impression."

He nodded, unoffended. "Third person, then, but in uniform."

"Yes, please," I said. "Would you be—hic—bringing a gun?"

"Dusenberry would have worn a sidearm. I usually carry a Navy revolver."

A whisper slid down my spine. I shook it off. The Navy revolver was a common choice, I reminded myself.

"That's fine, but please bring it unloaded."

Another nod. I began to think he was making a mental list. I revised my initial impression of him; he might look like a diminutive lumberjack, but I was getting the impression that he was a very intelligent individual.

"How long should I speak?" he asked.

"Fifteen or twenty minutes?" I said, looking to Willow for confirmation. "No more than half an hour."

"This will be at the end of the tour," Willow said, "so they'll be a little tired. Many of them will be along specifically to hear about Captain Dusenberry, though."

"Shouldn't be any problem," said Mr. Quentin. "I'll do a short talk and then answer questions. If you'll let me know what you'll be saying about the captain, Ms. Lane, I'll make sure to cover different points."

"That makes sense," Willow said.

"What would you charge for a half-hour talk?" I asked.

"Oh, there won't be any charge," he said. "I do this as educational outreach. I'll hand out a little flyer, if you don't mind." He reached into his coat pocket and produced a half-page flyer, neatly printed, promoting a local Civil War reenactor group.

"I don't mind at all, but do let me compensate you. We're talking about quite a few dates."

Willow took a folded page out of her purse and gave it to Mr. Quentin. "Here's the schedule. It's all the Wednesdays, Fridays, and Saturdays in October, plus two tours on Halloween. "

"I see," he said, studying the page. "I'll have to double-check that I'm available for all of these. May I keep this?"

"Yes, that's your copy," Willow said.

"Thank you." He bowed slightly in her direction, a gesture I found charmingly old-fashioned.

"If you'd prefer it, I can give you gift cards for afternoon tea as payment," I said, doing a quick mental calculation. "Say, one card for every two talks?"

His eyes lit with interest, and he turned to me with the first smile I'd seen from him and another bow. "I know several ladies who'd enjoy that. Thank you."

"Then it's a deal," I said, offering my hand.

He shook it, with a grip that was firm but not crushing. "It is a deal."

We chatted a little more, and Willow and Mr. Quentin exchanged cards. As I walked with them to the front door, Willow fell back beside me.

"We need to talk."

"I haven't heard back," I said.

At the door, I offered Mr. Quentin my hand, which he shook politely. "Thank you for coming in," I said. "I'm sure our customers will enjoy your talk very much."

He smiled, executed one of his small bows to me and another to Willow, and took his leave. Willow watched him go, looking thoughtful.

"Would you like a cup of tea?" I offered.

"I can't stay now," she said. "I have a tour in half an hour, but I could come back afterward, if that's all right. I do want to talk."

"That's fine," I said. "Four o'clock?"

"Four is perfect, thanks."

I saw her out, then went upstairs to my desk. Still no word from Tony. I sifted through the message slips and decided to call Bennett Cole at the Museum. He invited me to come by that afternoon and look at some Colt Navy revolvers, and since I was going to be out anyway, I agreed.

As I hung up, Kris came in, swinging a rather thin looking bank bag from her fingertips.

"Is there anything in it?" I asked.

"Yes. It's a slow week, though."

I stood and accepted the bag. "I'll be back in an hour or so. I'm st—hic—stopping by the museum. I'll have my cell if you need me."

"You driving?"

"No, I'll walk. It's not that heavy, and I like the rain."

"Have a nice walk. Don't catch cold."

In a few minutes I was stepping out the front door and taking a deep breath of rain-scented air. A whisper of smoke overlaid it from the fireplaces. My office and my suite would benefit from the heat going up the chimneys. I made a mental note to buy a cord of firewood for the winter, opened my umbrella, and headed out.

Pausing to look at my garden, I noted that it was time to go out with my shears and deadhead the roses. Chrysanthemums were blooming in the beds close by the house, and I smiled, remembering planting them a year ago. The garden was filling in nicely; still new, but no longer pitifully thin.

I thought about Nat and Manny's wedding, picturing where the ceremony would take place. We'd been going back and forth about a tent. There would be some shade from the trees to the south, and I wasn't sure that a tent big enough for the whole wedding would fit in my garden. Plus, I didn't know how one could be erected, unless it was put up in the neighboring parking lot and carried across the rosebushes. Standing umbrellas were a possible alternative. More discussion was in order.

I walked on, enjoying the novelty of a wet day in Santa Fe. Very few pedestrians. The cars were, of course, in a hurry, but on the whole it was a peaceful scene. There was no waiting in the bank, so I was just inside long enough to warm up, and then off again, swinging toward the Plaza and the Palace of the Governors on my way back.

Bennett Cole, a few years older than me and a few inches taller, with prematurely-thinning brown hair and a caterpillar mustache, was dressed for the chilly weather in a sweater vest over a work shirt and jeans. He welcomed me with a smile and led me downstairs into the Palace's basement, where I'd never been before. It was big—probably it ran under the entire Palace complex—and about as un-spooky as a basement could get. With fluorescent lighting and many steel cabinets of varying shapes and sizes, its atmosphere was closer to industrial than ancient.

Nevertheless, this was a treasure-hoard of New Mexico history. I knew that only a small percentage of the museum's collection of artifacts was on display at any given time. Knowing and seeing are two different things, though.

"Wow," I said. "I hadn't realized the collection was this big."

"This is only part of it," Bennett said, leading me to a tall standing cabinet. He pulled out a flat, shallow drawer in which lay half a dozen antique guns, all of the same size and shape. Some were in poor condition—pockmarked and showing signs of rust, the wooden handles partly decayed on a couple, one missing its trigger—though they were all clean.

"These are Colt Navy revolvers," Bennett said. "There were quite a lot of them in the territory around the time of the war."

They looked like classic cowboy guns, with big revolving cylinders and long barrels. Bennett picked one up and displayed it to me.

"See that design on it? That's why it's called a Navy revolver."

I peered at the cylinder where he indicated and saw a finely-engraved scene of a ship, with either clouds or explosions, I wasn't sure.

"Not because it was—hic—used by the Navy?" I asked.

"Right. Mostly it was used by civilians and soldiers. It was popular because it was lightweight, and could be carried easily in a holster."

"Lightweight?" I said, disbelieving.

"Compared to earlier revolvers, it was."

I gazed at it, thinking it looked deadly enough. Heavy enough, still, to kill if used as a club, never mind the bullets.

A weapon like this had killed Captain Dusenberry. Sudden sadness filled me.

I looked at the carefully-typed cards that lay in the drawer beside the guns. Some listed the original owners' names. Others confessed to a lack of knowledge about the items' past.

"I don't suppose any of these belonged to the hic— Hidalgos."

"Well, that's the disappointing news," said Bennett. "I checked our records. None of the Navy revolvers in our collection belonged to the Hidalgo family, that we know of. I'm sorry."

I inhaled deeply and nodded. Disappointing, but not surprising.

"That said," he added, "it's certainly possible that a Hidalgo owned one. It was a common gun."

"I see. Well, thanks."

"Any particular reason why you wanted to confirm that a Hidalgo owned a Navy revolver?"

"Well, it's the gun that killed Captain Dusenberry, I believe. Hic. And I've found some...information that implies the Hidalgos might not have been pleased with him."

I hadn't told Bennett about the stash of letters I'd found beneath the floor of my dining parlor. I knew I should; if I were virtuous, I'd donate the letters to the museum, but I felt reluctant to part with them. They were my link to Maria and the captain and their romance.

"Even if we could prove that a Hidalgo owned a Navy revolver," he said, "that wouldn't be enough to lay Dusenberry's murder at their door. There were just too many of the guns around."

"But if we did find a gun that belonged to the Hidalgos, wouldn't ballistics be able to match it to the bullet?"

"Maybe, if we had the bullet. As far as I know, we don't."

I nodded. "Well, thanks for your ti—hic—time."

"You're welcome. Good luck with your conundrum."

I glanced at him as we climbed the stairs back to the modern world, wondering why he'd chosen that word. He returned a grin, but didn't elaborate.

I walked home slowly. The rain had diminished to a faint drizzle, and for a few paces I left my umbrella closed, enjoying the moisture on my face.

Finally I shielded myself from further dampening, and sighed. I wasn't making much progress in solving Captain Dusenberry's murder. Or Daniel Swazo's, for that matter. For a corpse magnet, I was a pretty poor sleuth.

In both cases, I was somewhat at a loss to identify a killer. I had potential motive if the Hidalgos were indeed set against

Captain Dusenberry joining their illustrious family. But was murder really the only solution to that disagreement?

I wished, for perhaps the hundredth time, that I had Captain Dusenberry's side of the correspondence, not just Maria's. Sonja at the archives had come up blank when I'd asked her for Maria Hidalgo's papers. No doubt, Maria had either burned the captain's letters or hidden them so well they were as yet undiscovered.

A sudden desire to pull up the floor of the former Hidalgo hacienda gripped me. I suppressed it by shifting my thoughts to the more modern problem.

Why would anyone want to kill Daniel Swazo? Or, if they didn't actually want to kill him, why beat him up?

Something to do with the meth. But every time I tried to picture him involved with drugs, my mind rebelled. My knowledge of him was scant, but my instinct in this case was strong.

I knew very little about Daniel's community, or even his family. To learn more I'd have to go to the pueblo and ask nosy questions, and I hesitated to intrude on them that way. I could ask to visit Iz, but that would be imposing on her. It didn't feel right.

This wasn't my responsibility. Detective Walters would undoubtedly pester the people of Tesuque Pueblo more than enough. Maybe I could get Walters to share some of that information with me.

Fat chance.

It was almost four by the time I got back to the tearoom. I left my wet umbrella in the stand by the front door, hung my coat in the hall, and stepped into the gift shop, where Dee was helping a customer choose some leaf tea. Nat had stayed home because of the weather. I glanced at the reservation screen: the alcoves on the south side were all vacant. I could meet with Willow in Hyacinth, perhaps.

Hyacinth was one of two tiny alcoves adjacent to the gift shop. They might eventually go away, if adding the space to the shop would be more profitable than keeping it for guests—a complicated equation on which Kris had been working for a month or so. But for now, they stayed, set off by screens and sharing the fireplace, which currently held the embers of a lovely fire. Hyacinth would be cozy.

No, Violet. Willow would want to see the tribute to Vi. And we might talk about things that I wouldn't want anyone in the gift shop to overhear.

Dee's customers departed. I asked her to bring cream tea for two to Violet at four o'clock. She checked her watch.

"That's in five minutes."

"Right, so you'd better get—hic—started. I'll keep watch in case anyone comes in to browse."

Dee headed for the pantry, and I made a quick visit to the main parlor. One nice, older couple from Michigan sat in Lily; I chatted with them briefly and learned that this was their first time in Santa Fe. I made a couple of recommendations about things to see, then left them enjoying their tea.

The only other party was a pair of young women in Iris, who were so deeply engrossed in conversation that I decided not to intrude on them. I headed back to the gift shop.

The front door opened as I crossed the hall. It was Willow, wearing a black raincoat sprinkled with moisture. I led her back to Violet, where Dee had been quick to set two places for tea.

"This is lovely," Willow said as she removed the raincoat. "You've redone it."

"Let me take that for you. Yes, we wanted to honor Vi."

She nodded. "The portrait is perfect."

I stepped into the hall to hang up Willow's coat. The shop was still empty, so I snagged a fresh log from the holder in Hyacinth and returned to Violet, whose fireplace (shared with Dahlia) was back to back with the front one. One large chimney served both sides, and the same arrangement was reflected on the north side of the house, with a single chimney serving fireplaces in the main parlor and the dining parlor.

Willow had made herself comfortable in one of the wing

chairs in Violet. The embers in the fireplace matched those on the other side; I added the log and poked the fire back to life.

"I haven't heard back from Detective Aragón," I said, taking the other chair.

Willow leaned forward, reaching her hands toward the fire. "I've been thinking about what you told me, about Daniel Swazo."

"Oh?" I glanced toward the gift shop, trusting that no one was there to hear.

She lowered her voice so that I could barely hear her. "I don't believe knives are generally used in the preparation of meth for consumption."

"Pardon?"

"I'm not an expert, but one hears about 'cutting' cocaine. Not so much with meth, I think. You could ask the detective. What I'm getting at is that it's unusual to have found meth on the knife. For one thing, I would think it wouldn't stick."

"Maybe their tests are ve—hic—very sensitive."

"Maybe. But why would a meth user handle the drug that way?"

"I have no idea." I tried to think of a different subject. Talking about the knife was making me really uncomfortable.

"Well, neither have I," Willow said. "It's been bothering me. It doesn't fit."

Dee came in with a pot of tea and a small tray of scones with clotted cream and lemon curd. "Thank you, Dee," I said as she poured for us.

She gave me a fleeting smile and left. Willow picked up her teacup. "This is lovely, thanks."

"Perfect on a rainy day," I said, adding a dollop of milk to my cup.

"Yes. I could get addicted to tea."

"I already am."

"Speaking of addictions, I don't think Daniel was a drug user," she added, helping herself to a scone.

"I don't think so either."

"Which means it fits even less."

I sighed. "There's something I'm not understanding. That's why I keep ha—hic—ving these dreams."

"Yes. Daniel believes you can help him."

"Help him what? Isn't he finished with this world?"

Concern darkened her eyes. "He should be, yes, But there's something he hasn't let go of. I'm afraid I don't understand it myself. He's quite focused on you."

Great. I poured myself more tea, and added a lump of sugar this time.

Do me a favor, Daniel. If you have something to say, tell it to Willow. She's listening.

"I'll let you know as soon as I hear back from Detective Aragón," I said.

Willow nodded. "Meanwhile, you might talk to Daniel before you go to sleep."

Are you kidding me?

I managed not to say that aloud. Instead, I said, "Wouldn't that make me more likely to dream about him?"

"Actually, no. If he's using dreams to communicate with you, then by telling him you haven't forgotten when you go to bed, you might get him to leave you alone."

I took a scone and pulled it in half, then put curd and cream on one side. "Worth a try, I guess."

"You don't like it, I know," she said softly, "but it's really an honor to be contacted by a spirit. It isn't easy for them."

I had no answer for that, so I took a bite of my scone. It seemed easy enough for Captain Dusenberry, given how often he'd made his presence known. Maybe I'd taken that for granted.

"What did you think of Mr. Quentin?" I asked, wanting to change the subject.

"I liked him. He seemed very respectful. I think he'll do a good job."

"I hope these tours will be worth the effort."

"I think they will be. I'm already getting reservations. I took the liberty of posting the dates on my website."

"Have you? I'll get you a copy of the ad I'll be running."

"Thanks."

"Do you want candles? Just a couple, on the dining table?"

"That would be nice."

We chatted a bit more, until the tea and the scones were gone. I offered to brew more tea, but Willow shook her head.

"I'd better be going. This was lovely, thank you. What do I owe?"

I shook my head. "It's on the house. This was a consultation."

She gave me an amused smile, and I realized that could be taken more than one way.

"About the tours," I specified.

"Of course. I'll be in touch."

I saw her out, then returned to Violet to find Dee already clearing the dishes. She looked up. "Ellen?"

I paused. Dee straightened, tea tray in hand, and pressed her lips together. Her expression was intent, made the more so by her black-framed glasses. "I just wanted to apologize. We shouldn't have tried to scare you."

"Oh." I waved a dismissive hand. "Don't worry about it."

"No, it was wrong. We were out of line. It was my idea, not Mick's. He's worried you're mad."

"I'm not—hic—mad. I'm just a bit tired is all." I smiled to reassure her, then went upstairs, collecting my coat from the hall.

I emerged at the top of the stairs into a peaceful silence. Kris had gone home for the day, judging from the quiet and from the three message slips on my desk: one from Nat, one from a supplier, and one from Detective Walters. The latter made my stomach surge, even though the only message was a request that I call him back.

I glanced at the clock, decided I was off work and wouldn't see that message until the morning, and laid the empty bank bag on Kris's desk. There was no message from Tony. I'd give him another day, and if I still didn't hear from him I'd find a way to ask him about it on Saturday, when he brought his family to tea. My stomach gave a little nervous flutter at the thought.

Remembering my promise to myself, I fetched my current book from my suite and retreated to the chaise longue by the nicely-baking chimney. I stayed there until 6:00, when I heard footsteps on the stairs.

"Ellen?" Dee's voice came through my open door. "We're going."

I got up and went out to acknowledge her. She was standing at the top of the stairs, a long coat over her lavender dress, a scarf around her neck and a jaunty beret on her head.

"Thanks," I said. "I'll walk down with you."

"I banked the fires and locked everything up," she told me.

I nodded, and continued down the stairs beside her. She'd mentioned her brother was worrying, and I wanted to set him at ease.

Mick was waiting by the back door, a navy-colored hoodie covering his pale hair. He hastily pulled out his earbuds when he saw me.

"Good night," I told him, smiling. "See you both tomorrow."

An answering smile flicked across his face, though his eyes still watched me warily.

"Night," Dee said, fishing her keys out of her purse.

I watched them away, then did my own final check. The kitchen was spotless; china not only clean but all put away. The parlors were tidy, ready for the morning. The fires in all the fireplaces—front and back of each chimney—were down to coals and were safely banked.

The lights were on in the dining parlor. I turned them off and headed back upstairs. Before I was halfway up, the stereo came on.

I paused, debating whether this was a major message or just a hello. The latter, I decided. It was a random track from the music that played during the day. I went back down and shut off the stereo.

"Thank you," I said aloud, "but I think I'd rather have quiet."

I waited, listening, but the music did not come back on. Apparently Captain Dusenberry understood.

8

AFTER MEASURING EXACTLY three eighths of a sleeping pill, and (feeling like an idiot) telling Daniel I hadn't forgotten about the knife, I managed to get a fairly good night's sleep. I still hiccuped. I still dreamed: disturbing dreams, but the kind one doesn't remember, much less wake from with a scream.

Midway through the morning I got a text from Tony:

Check your email

He had forwarded a copied-and-pasted section of the lab report on the knife. I puzzled over a list of chemical terms. Apparently meth wasn't the only thing they'd found on the blade, but I might as well have tried to read Greek as to understand the results.

Well, Latin.

I tried searching on some of the terms. Methamphetamine hydrochloride...that would be the meth. Ferulic acid had something to do with plants. At pronyl-lysine, my eyes started to cross.

Tony had carefully removed the description of the knife itself, except for the word "blade." What was left was just a list of the components found on it. If I asked for help with the terms, I didn't think that would be a violation of his confidence.

I printed out the list and carried it downstairs. Rosa and Iz were in the pantry, their dark heads bent together as they talked. They both straightened when I came in, making me think of maids snapping to attention in some British drama. I coughed to hide a laugh.

"Either of you study chemistry?" I asked.

They both shook their heads. Iz was taking college courses,

but from her expression I gathered she had some other major.

I went through to the kitchen, where Mick was just firing up the dishwashing station to work on the day's first round of china. He politely removed his earbuds when I went up to him, but denied any knowledge of chemistry.

I turned to Julio and Ramon, who were working on savory pies. Julio shook his head without looking up from rolling the dough.

"Just kitchen chemistry," he said. "I can tell you about leavening agents."

"Pronyl-lysine?"

"No way."

Ramon answered my look with a shrug. "He's the smart one," he said, nodding toward Julio. "I'm just a guitarist."

"You're not 'just' a guitarist," I said. "Music is one of the highest arts."

He gave me an appreciative grin. "Yeah, but it ain't chemistry."

Discouraged, I went back through the pantry and headed down the main hall to the gift shop. Dee was there, ringing up a sale for a customer. Nat stood at the podium, looking sharp in a rust-colored dress and a turquoise necklace.

"Did you ta—hic—take chemistry in school?" I asked her quietly.

"Not if I could help it."

"Hm."

I studied the list again. It still looked pretty meaningless to me.

Dee's customer concluded her purchase and walked past me on her way out, smiling. Dee sidled up to the podium and glanced at my list.

"Oh—is that a chemical analysis?"

"Yes," I said, my heart giving a small hop of hope. "Can you understand it?"

She took the page from my hand, frowning. "We had a little of this in my forensics class. Oh, that's m—" She stopped herself, glanced toward the hall, and lowered her voice. "That's meth!"

"Do you know what any of the others are?" I asked.

"Ferulic acid is plant-based." She tilted her head, frowning at the words. "Hmm. Glutenin, starch—this sounds like food."

"Food?"

Four ladies walked into the gift shop, laughing together. Dee handed me back the list and went to attend to them. I stuffed the page in my pocket, then headed upstairs.

Food on the knife. Maybe Daniel had been using it to eat?

And then to have some meth for dessert?

My mind rejected that. I didn't think Daniel was a drug user. My encounter with him had been brief, but he hadn't given me that impression at all. Also, Iz had said he wasn't into drugs.

I looked in on Kris, who was on the phone. As I stepped back she picked up her empty teacup and gave me a hopeful smile. I took it from her, but the teapot on the credenza was empty.

Downstairs again, to the pantry. I made a pot of Assam because it was fast-brewing, and hurried back up to give Kris her cuppa.

She was off the phone. "Thanks," she said, closing her eyes as she inhaled the steam gently rising from her cup. "Keemun?"

"Assam."

"I knew it was one or the other." She took a swallow. "I just got a quote on a 3-D printer."

"Oh?"

"You're not going to like it."

She handed me a slip of paper. I read the numbers and winced. "We can't do it."

"Not this year."

"Well, I did tell Julio not to get his hopes up. I'll ho—hic—hold onto this." I started for my office, then remembered the analysis. "I don't suppose you know chemistry?"

Kris slowly shook her head, watching me with wide, dark eyes. I stifled a sigh and went back to my desk, collecting a cup of tea for myself along the way.

There, on top of the stack of lavender slips, was the message from Detective Walters. I grimaced and took a swallow of tea. Decided it needed sugar and milk, if I was going to call the detective back. I picked up my cup and headed for the tea tray.

I knew I was procrastinating. I stood by the credenza, stirring my modified tea and thinking. What could Walters want now?

I went back and looked through the rest of the messages. Made a call to my doctor's office requesting an appointment. The earliest they could see me was Wednesday.

Remembering that it was Willow who had asked for more details about the knife, I forwarded the chemical analysis to her. Unless she had credentials I didn't know about—or some kind of ghostly consultant—it wouldn't mean much to her, either, but at least she'd know I'd kept my promise.

Finally out of delaying tactics, I dialed Walters's number. I silently cheered when I got his voicemail. Leaving a brief, polite message, I turned to the rest of my chores.

The day went by swiftly, as Fridays tended to do at the tearoom. Better weather brought out more customers, and the weekends were always our busiest days. I spent the evening reading and went to bed early, hoping to be fresh for my tea with Tony and his family. With the aid of a partial pill I again slept well, although I did dream about giant pillars of striped turquoise, malachite, and sugilite.

Saturday morning I woke to the smell of almond cake baking downstairs. A sense of peace and well-being filled me. I lay in bed drowsing, telling myself I'd get up in a couple of minutes, enjoying a last bit of laziness before facing the day. Maybe the piece of pill I'd taken was a little too large. Maybe I'd sleep another five minutes.

I hiccuped, bursting the hope that I'd finally kicked the spasms. Sighing, I threw the covers aside and got up. A glance out the window showed me a sunny morning, but with puffs of cloud already gathering. By afternoon, it might rain.

I breakfasted on berries and yogurt, and took a quick shower. Choosing a dress to wear, since I was having tea with Tony and his family, took longer than usual. Not too fancy—I didn't want to appear to be flaunting my prosperity—but not too causal either. This was a formal first meeting, in a formal setting, and I wanted to pay due respect to Tony's elders. I ended up choosing a pale green silk dress with a high neck, trimmed with narrow lace at the hem and cuffs. I piled my hair on top of my head, letting a couple of strategic wisps hang curling, and took extra care with my makeup.

Before leaving my suite, I checked my phone. No messages, no texts. I texted Tony.

> Thank you for the report. Looking forward to this afternoon.

Crossing the hall to my office, I waved good morning to Kris, who was on the phone. My desk was clear of message slips for the moment. I left my cell phone there and headed downstairs. The tearoom wouldn't open for a couple of hours, but the day would be busy; about three quarters of our available seating was booked, and there were always walk-ins on Saturdays.

Rosa had just arrived and was studying the reservations chart, loading a tray with china and silver and linens. I put a kettle on to boil, then looked in on the kitchen, where Julio was showing Ramon how to pipe buttercream icing wisteria blossoms—beautifully shaded from palest lavender to violet—onto dainty, iced petit fours. Ramon, frowning with concentration, spared me only a brief glance.

"Morning, boss," Julio said absently. I didn't correct him; he was good about calling me Ellen rather than "boss" in public situations.

"Good morning. Anything you n—hic—need for today?"

"We're good. Thanks."

"I, ah...have some special guests today."

Julio shot me a sidelong glance. "The Aragóns? I might have something extra for them. I'm experimenting with a new sweet, a chocolate pot de crème in a meringue cup. You eat the custard, then eat the cup."

"Sounds like Willy Wonka. I thought pots de crème were

baked in a water bath."

"Well, yeah. That part's going to be different."

"Will they break?"

"The meringue cups? I hope not. That's why it's an experiment."

"All right. I'll just warn them. Thanks."

Returning to the pantry just as the kettle boiled, I started a pot of tea brewing, then walked down the hall to the main parlor where Rosa was setting up the alcoves for the first guests of the day. I glanced at the fresh flowers in every vase, and pulled one slightly faded bloom from a spray of alstroemeria in Lily. Rosa looked up at me from arranging a place setting and grinned.

"Big day today," she said.

I smiled back, but didn't comment. I didn't want to betray how nervous I felt.

Returning to the pantry, I retrieved my tea and headed upstairs. As I emerged into the hall, the back door opened and Dee and Mick came in.

"Morning," I said to them, smiling. "You're early."

"Iz and I switched," Dee said, pulling off her beret and gloves. "She had something to do this morning. Hope that's OK."

Instantly I knew what the something was: Daniel Swazo's funeral. I'd seen the notice and thought about going, but I didn't actually know Daniel, and however sympathetic I might feel toward him, those who knew him might not like to be around the person who found his body. A wave of sadness went through me.

"That's fine," I said, and turned to the stairs.

Kris was still on the phone. I poured tea for us both, then retreated to my desk.

Poor Daniel. His bruised and swollen face, unrecognizable, brushed through my memory.

I had a small candle holder on my desk, shaped like a water lily, just big enough for a tea light. I put a fresh candle in, lit it, and silently wished him peaceful rest.

Willow's words about Daniel came back to me. There was

something he wanted to accomplish, something about his knife, and he wouldn't rest until it was done. Had I done all I could in that direction? I hadn't heard back from Willow about the report, but then I really hadn't expected to. She might not be able to make any more of it than I could.

Thinking about Daniel made me restless. Maybe I should go back to the flea market and see if anything there pointed me toward a knot I could unravel. I couldn't go today; it would have to wait until tomorrow, Sunday, when the tearoom would be closed. Nat and I were planning to work on the dresses again, but I could go to the market before I went to her place.

Sunday. One week after Daniel's death. They said that if a killer wasn't found in the first few days, the chances of finding him/her diminished.

Had Daniel been murdered, though? Or was his death the result of a random fight that had nothing to do with his knife or the meth? Maybe it was just a tragic accidental death, caused by a blow that wasn't meant to be fatal.

But if that was so, why was I dreaming about Daniel and his knife?

"Meditating?"

I looked up from the candle at Kris, who stood in the doorway, her purple-and-black striped floor-length sundress a last farewell to summer. She'd be cold, later, if it rained.

"Just musing," I said. "Do you need me?"

"Gina Fiorelli just sent me an email asking if we wanted to see designs for holiday ads."

I whispered an unladylike word. Gina's company's rates were higher than I could really afford, but the last time I'd hired somebody cheaper I hadn't been happy with the results. I knew Gina would cut me a break, but I didn't like taking advantage of our friendship that way.

"Yes, we do," I said, giving in. "Figure out what we can afford and give her a budget. Send her the details about the Halloween spirit tour and tea combos, too. Did I forward that to you?"

"No."

"I'll do it now."

"What about December? Are we going to have a holiday special?"

"I don't know. I'll think about it. We can start with something generic, like 'Celebrate the holidays,' blah, blah, blah."

"OK."

"And Kris—"

She paused in the doorway, stunning, as always. Her eyes looked almost violet. A trick of her clothing.

"Thank you."

A corner of her mouth curved upward. "I know you don't like dealing with ads."

"That, my dear, is an understatement."

She grinned and retreated to her office. I hunted through my correspondence with Willow and collected the details for the tea tour combo—there had to be a more graceful name—and emailed it all to Kris. That done, I looked through my email and messages and dealt with a couple of other tasks. Nothing from Tony.

Looking back at the candle flame, I finished the last of my tea, then got up. I made certain the candle was away from anything flammable, left my teacup on the credenza, and went back downstairs.

Rosa and Dee were putting the finishing touches on the alcoves. China and silver gleamed on the low tables, and white linens blossomed at each place setting. Rosa had found a book about folding napkins a couple of weeks before, and the servers had been playing with different styles from it. Today the napkins were rosettes, nestled in the teacups.

I poked my head into the kitchen. Not a petit four in sight. Ramon had moved on to making cucumber sandwiches, and Julio was putting trays of scones into the oven. I glanced at the clock: almost ten. We'd be open in half an hour.

Nat had arrived, wearing a blue and green flowered dress. She looked up from helping Dee tidy the displays in the gift shop, and greeted me with a smile. "You look lovely, dear! When is your party?"

"It's Tony's party, not mine. Two o'clock."

"It'll be splendid."

"I hope so."

I had seated us in the Jonquil alcove, thinking Tony would prefer to have a view of the street. There was a party booked there for 11:30, which should leave plenty of time to reset the alcove for the Aragóns.

The thought came to me that I didn't know whether Tony's grandmother was an Aragón or a maternal grandmother. The fact that she was coming with Tony's mother implied the latter. Mrs. Aragón was a hairdresser, I knew. Tony had never mentioned his father. That was the sum total of what I knew about his parentage, other than the fact that his grandparents (maternal? I wasn't sure) had lost their ancestral home because of their inability to pay Santa Fe's steep property taxes.

Anxiety threatened; I fought it by distracting myself, making another round of the parlors and visiting the kitchen once more. Julio handed me a small plate bearing six perfect fresh raspberries.

"Go have a cup of tea," he said. "Everything's fine. Looks like the meringues are going to work."

"Oh, good. Thank you. Hic."

He nodded, then tilted his head. "You gonna see a doctor about that, boss?"

"I have an appointment next week."

I got out of his way, snagged a cup of tea from the servers' pot because the tea upstairs would be cold, and went up to my office to give the raspberries due attention. They were my favorite fruit, and I ate them one at a time, savoring their sweetness and the sensual texture of the seeds.

When they were gone, I closed my eyes and took a deep breath. I was not much given to prayer, but I made a silent wish that all would go well with Tony's family. I sat still, with the ghost of raspberries on my tongue, picturing a happy meeting, until I hiccuped.

Opening my eyes, I reached for my cell phone. No answer from Tony. The time showed 10:35. We were open.

I went back downstairs and made an effort to keep myself busy. There was plenty to do: helping out in the gift shop and the butler's pantry, supporting the servers, greeting guests. At 1:45 I darted up to my suite to touch up my hair and makeup. As I was coming down the stairs, I met the Bird Woman.

She was headed for the dining parlor, burdened with her gigantic purse and a large orange-and-pink gift bag, leading a handful of her friends. It was not a Red Hat day; instead perched atop her head was a confection of white gauze, silver ribbon, and pale yellow feathers that was rather too ethereal for her yellow-and-white polka dot dress. A feathery shawl draped over her elbows, and her hands were encased in crocheted gloves. Combined with her bright, bird-like eyes, the ensemble reminded me forcibly of a cockatiel.

"What a magnificent hat," was all I could think to say.

She beamed. "I just got it. I found this great website, Victorian Fantasies. You should check it out."

"I will." I stepped toward the dining parlor, encouraging her to follow so that her party wouldn't block the hallway. "Are you ladies celebrating something special today?"

"It's Sally's birthday," said the Bird Woman, turning to grin at one of her friends, a shy-looking woman wearing a lime-green cloche hat over her short gray curls.

I smiled. "Happy Birthday, then, and many happy returns."

"See? I told you she's got a fancy way with words," said the Bird Woman. She turned to me. "Hey, you find any more deaders?"

"No," I said firmly, then hiccuped.

We were at the door to the parlor. I invited them to go in with a gesture, then escaped through the pantry to the kitchen, biting back my annoyance. I counted to ten before speaking.

"Julio? The party in the dining parlor is celebrating a birthday."

"Yeah, they ordered a cake. It's ready."

"Send them something special, if there's anything they ha—hic—haven't ordered."

"Will do."

"Thank you."

I blinked, trying to recover my composure. The Bird Woman had an uncanny ability to rattle me, and not just by mentioning corpses.

I looked at the kitchen clock. Ten minutes to two. Taking a deep breath and letting it out slowly, I headed back out to the hallway. Dee was just leaving the pantry carrying a tray of teapots; she glanced at me as she crossed to the dining parlor. I gave her a nod, then continued toward the front of the tearoom, reminding myself to smile.

Iz was leading a nicely-dressed blonde couple into the parlor as I headed for the gift shop. The gentleman, dapper in a linen suit, paused.

"Ellen?"

I turned and found myself face to face with Loren Jackson. I'd never seen him dressed up. His well-tailored suit showed off trim shoulders I'd only partly been aware of, and his soft green necktie was perfectly knotted. A familiar, woodsy fragrance teased the edge of my awareness. A smile lit his face, and my stomach surprised me by tightening.

"M-may I introduce my sister?" he asked. "Shelly, this is the owner of the tearoom, Ellen Rosings."

I turned to her with an automatic smile. She was as fair as her brother, pale blond hair clustering around her face in soft curls. Her periwinkle dress made her blue eyes seem unusually large.

"How do you do?" I said, offering to shake hands. "Welcome to the Wisteria Tearoom."

"Thank you." She smiled, a little shyly. "When I heard Loren had been here I made him bring me. I've been curious."

"And I wanted to come as a patron," Loren added, a bit hastily. "I've admired the building since I first saw it, and I—I wanted to spend some time here."

Shelly turned an inquiring look on him. "I thought she was a friend of yours."

"Actually, she's a client," he said.

"Well, you certainly chose a beautiful day to vi—hic—visit." I glanced at Iz with a slight nod. "I hope you have a lovely tea."

Iz stepped into the main parlor, guiding them toward the Rose alcove. Loren paused, gazing at me with an expression of concern.

Yes, I still have the hiccups.

I managed a smile, then turned to the gift shop, suppressing dismay. Why had Loren chosen to bring his sister here today, of all days? They'd be within earshot of me and the Aragóns.

Not that I thought they would eavesdrop. What did it matter?

I needed to sort my thoughts. Hyacinth was unoccupied; I slipped into the alcove and sat in a plush chair, trying to understand my reaction to the Jacksons. I hadn't expected to see Loren, but surprise alone couldn't account for the way their appearance had thrown me off balance.

Was it concern that Loren would speak of things I'd told him in confidence? No. I trusted him.

I thought of the Aragóns, and the reason clicked into focus. I was worried that Tony would be jealous.

Absurd. I had seen Loren only on a professional basis. I'd gone to him for counseling. There was no reason at all for Tony to be jealous.

Except, perhaps, the warmth in Loren's eyes.

Oh, I needed to figure that out...and figure out how I felt about it...and I didn't have time.

I checked my watch. Almost two.

Later. I'd deal with it later. Loren and his sister would be settled by now. I'd just focus all my attention on Tony and his elders, and all would be well.

I rose, smoothed my dress, and stepped out into the gift shop just as the bells on the front door tinkled. A pretty Hispanic woman stepped into the hallway and held the door open for two more ladies, both older than she. One was middle-aged, her glossy hair looking fresh from the beautician's hands. She assisted the third, whose equally-styled silver hair set off a pair of deep-set, rather fierce eyes. This lady leaned on an aluminum walker and took tiny shuffling steps, pausing to lift her feet over the threshold with great care. They all wore nice dresses and modest jewelry.

Nat was helping a customer, and the servers were all elsewhere. I stepped forward.

"Good afternoon," I said, smiling. "How may I help you?"

The youngest woman looked at me, hesitating briefly before speaking. "We have a reservation. Aragón."

"Oh!" I looked from her to the other two ladies. "We weren't expecting three. That is—hic—"

"My brother was supposed to be here, but he had to work."

Disappointment and realization washed through me together. At least Tony had made arrangements for his family to keep their reservation.

"Oh, I see. I'm Ellen Rosings," I explained, offering a hand.

The youngest woman shook it in a feather-light grasp. She was a few years younger than I, and seemed a bit tense. "I'm Angela, Tony's sister."

"I'm delighted to meet you." I smiled, turning to the others. "And you must be Tony's mother and grandmother."

Angela hastened to introduce me to her mother, Dolores, and her grandmother, Theresa. A faint aura of cigarette smoke clung to them; I remembered that Tony had said his grandmother smoked. I welcomed them and led them to the Jonquil alcove. As Dolores was settling her mother in an emerald green wing chair, I spoke softly to Angela.

"I was going to join you, but—"

"Oh, please don't go away. Tony said he wanted you to get acquainted with them." She gestured to her family with a worried glance.

"All right."

I stepped to the window to adjust the lace sheers. The sun

wasn't coming in at the moment, but it might before we finished our tea.

Angela and her mother had seated themselves on the settee, leaving me the other chair. Angela's pink sun-dress and ivory wrap looked spring-like against the settee's pale yellow velvet. Dolores's dress was a sober navy that I could easily picture her wearing to church. Theresa's was a muted print of red and orange flowers, less flamboyant than the Bird Woman's usual attire, but perhaps a more subtle expression of the same devil-may-care attitude. She fixed me with a stony gaze.

"So you are the girl Antonio has been seeing."

Angela made a small, dismayed sound. Dolores leaned forward.

"Mama," she said, and added a string of Spanish too rapid for me to follow.

Iz came into the alcove with a teapot on a tray. "Good afternoon," she said softly. "Welcome to the Wisteria Tearoom."

We were silent as Iz poured the tea. I noticed that Angela sat stiffly erect, perched on the edge of her seat. Poised to flee, perhaps?

Iz put the teapot on its tray, covered it with a cozy printed with yellow and white jonquils, and murmured a promise that she'd be back soon with our food. As she left, I selected a lump of sugar from the bowl and slipped it into my cup.

"I'm so sorry Detective Aragón couldn't join us," I said, stirring my tea. "I suppose he couldn't get away—hic—from work?"

"Yes," Angela said hastily, watching her mother hold the sugar bowl for her grandmother, who gripped the tongs with wiry fingers and dropped three lumps of sugar into her cup. "He said to apologize."

"No need. I understand perfectly."

"It was very nice of you to invite us," Dolores said, returning the sugar bowl to the table.

"Well, I owed your son a thank-you," I said. "He's helped me a great deal."

"You took him to the Opera," said Theresa, in a tone that bordered on accusatory.

I turned to her with what I hoped was a calm smile. "Yes, he was kind enough to escort me to a friend's party. I'm afraid he—hic—ended up working that night, too."

Iz returned with a three-tiered tea tray, which she set in the center of the table. Theresa's eyes lit with interest at the sight of the food, making me glad that I had ordered a full afternoon tea service for the party. I watched her and the others covertly as Iz briefly explained the menu. When she departed, the Aagóns sat frozen, staring at the tea tray as if unsure what to do with it.

I took out the plate of savories and offered it to Theresa. She helped herself to one of each item, placing them on her plate with fingers that wavered only slightly.

Moving the savories to within Dolores's reach, I looked at Angela. "Are you the sister who's in college?"

"Yes. I'm studying to be a nurse."

"I admire you. That's hard work."

She nodded seriously. "There's a nursing shortage, so I should be able to get a job."

Something in her tone made me think that getting a good job was a matter of urgency for her. I was suddenly conscious of the opulence of our surroundings. The furnishings and draperies, the fine china, the tearoom itself—all were expensive. I was still paying off the cost of equipping the tearoom, and of course the mortgage would go on for decades. Sitting with the Aragóns, I was reminded of how fortunate I was to be able to carry the debt.

Tony had sneered, when we first met. Not because I was Anglo—well, maybe partly because of that—but mostly because I owned this house. Because I had money.

I'd never thought of myself as rich. The advantages I'd had growing up—music lessons, travel, then college—were all things I had taken for granted. Until I'd met Tony.

As I held the plate of savories for Angela to help herself, I glanced at her grandmother and saw the same defiant pride in her face that I had first seen in Tony's. She might not have as much cash, but she considered herself as good as me or better. And she didn't think I was good enough for her grandson, I suspected.

The remaining savories were mine. I put them on my plate, returned the empty serving plate to the tea tray, and took a bite of my cucumber sandwich, wondering how I would get through the next hour.

Loren Jackson's laughter carried to me from the Rose alcove. He and his sister must be sharing some joke. At least I wouldn't have to worry about an encounter between him and Tony.

"Where are you studying?" I asked Angela, for lack of a better conversational gambit.

I listened to her talk about her classes, my thoughts partly on Tony. Maybe he'd had a breakthrough in his case. I hoped so.

I became aware that Dolores was addressing me, just in time to register that she was asking me where I'd gone to school. She smiled politely; she was trying to help me.

"UNM," I said. "I considered some other schools, but decided I di—hic—didn't want to go far from home."

"And you have a degree?"

"I have a bachelor's in music and a master's in literature. Not very practical, I'm afraid."

Dolores seemed to have nothing to say to that. She sipped her tea.

Reminded of my duties as hostess, I lifted the tea cozy from the pot and made sure everyone's cup was full. Theresa gave me a regal nod of acknowledgment as I poured for her. She was making inroads on her savories.

Surely she could not be going hungry at home; they weren't that poor. More likely, she hadn't encountered some of these foods before, and had a healthy appetite for variety.

"The *empanadas* are very good," she said, brandishing half a Cornish pasty.

I didn't correct her; the difference was unimportant. Far more important was her enjoyment of the meal.

"Thank you. I'm glad you like it. Would you like a scone?

These are British style, not as heavy as American."

As I offered her the breads plate, I gave myself a mental swat. She might never have had any scones, British or American. Tony hadn't been familiar with them before I served them to him. I took a scone myself and tore it open, spreading lemon curd and clotted cream on each half. Dolores and Angela watched, then helped themselves.

"You must like the English very much," Dolores said, and gestured to our surroundings. "To do all this."

"Yes, I've always been an Anglophile. My mother was, too, and I grew up watching all the BBC shows on Channel Five."

"And that's what made you want to have a tea room?" Angela asked.

"Well, partly. I've always loved tea." I decided not to mention my trip to England with my parents. "It was my aunt who suggested that I open a tearoom. I was very depressed after my father died, and she knew that having something to work toward would help me sna—hic—snap out of it. I do apologize...these stupid hiccups..." I rubbed my forehead, suddenly weary.

"Have you had them all day?" Angela asked.

"All week."

"You've had the hiccups all week?" Dolores looked at me as if I was nuts.

I waved a hand, trying to dismiss the subject. "It's just been a tough week."

"Drink some water with a pencil in your mouth," said Theresa.

I blinked at her. "What?"

Theresa nodded firmly, then picked up her spoon and demonstrated. "Like a pirate biting his knife—so. Then get a glass of water and drink it."

I'd heard plenty of odd suggestions in the past few days, but this was odder than most.

"Well...it's worth a try," I said gamely. "Thank you."

"If that doesn't work, you might want to see a doctor," Angela suggested gently.

"I have an appointment," I said.

An awkward silence followed. The Aragóns were embarrassed to be having tea with a defective human who couldn't even rid herself of the hiccups.

I took a deep breath and turned to Dolores. "Your hair is lovely, Mrs. Aragón. I think Tony mentioned you have a salon?"

"I don't own one. I work in one."

"Ah."

Defective *and* tactless. Would I never learn?

"What are those?" demanded Theresa, a bony finger pointing at the strawberry puffs on the sweets plate. I removed the plate from the tea tray and offered it to her.

"Meringues with strawberry cream. Try one."

I handed the sweets to Dolores once Theresa had claimed her share. She and Angela took one of each. My plate didn't have room for sweets; I'd fallen behind. To be honest, I wasn't very hungry.

I made myself take a bite of scone. It tasted like sawdust. I knew that it was me, not the scone, that was the problem. I was sliding into a blue funk.

No matter how hard I tried, I couldn't guarantee that things would go perfectly. Tony's absence had really thrown me, more than it should have. I'd been counting on him to help me get acquainted with his family. Without him, I was awkward and embarrassed.

Which was ridiculous. Since when did I depend on the presence of Tony Aragón for my own poise? I raised my head and sat straighter in my chair.

"Tony's older than you, right?" I said to Angela.

"A few years older, yes."

I tried to remember whether Tony and I had talked about college. My impression was that he hadn't gone—perhaps because there had been no money. Did he go straight into the police academy?

"I was wondering why he chose to go into police work," I said. "I don't believe he's mentioned the reason to me."

Angela looked at her mother, who was suddenly interested in her sweets. "Our father was a policeman," she said.

"Oh?"

"He was killed on duty."

My throat tightened. "I'm so sorry. Was it recent?"

Angela shook her head. "Tony was seventeen. I was twelve." Again, she looked at her mother. Following her gaze, I saw that Dolores was plainly still grieving.

It had to have been ten years, or nearly so. My heart clenched with sympathetic pain. My father had been gone for two years. My mother six. It still hurt.

"So he inspired Tony to follow in his career?" I said. "He must have been a ve—hic—very good father."

Dolores raised her head, looking at me with eyes every bit as fierce as Theresa's. "He was a good man."

I felt I was digging myself deeper into a conversational pit. Soon I'd be able to pull the sides in after myself.

"I'm so sorry for your loss," I said softly.

Dolores's eyes flashed with passion, then she looked down at her plate once more. She picked up her teacup, which was empty.

I reached for the pot and poured the last of the tea into Dolores's cup. I was tempted to go fetch more myself, just for the sake of a moment alone, but it would be rude to abandon my guests, and I would have to pass the Jacksons. Not wise.

Instead, I tipped the lid of the teapot and waited for Iz to come by and notice.

"You going to eat your strawberry?" Theresa said to me.

I shook my head, suppressed a hiccup, and offered her the sweets plate again. She took the strawberry puff, and her hand hovered over the petit four as she glanced at me. I nodded, and she cleared the plate.

Well, at least one of us was having a good time.

I tried to think of a safe topic to introduce, but all my usual polite inquiries had so far led to disaster. Probably I'd be better off keeping my mouth shut. There were times when even Miss Manners couldn't help me.

"Everything is good," Theresa said, and licked a bit of cream from her fingers.

"Thank you." I assumed it was high praise. Grandmothers have no obligation to give polite compliments.

"Do you cook everything yourself?" Angela asked, and I recognized an attempt to help.

Grateful, I smiled, shaking my head. "No, we have a chef. Julio Delgado. He's much more talented in the kitchen than I am."

Dolores looked up. "Anna Delgado's father?"

"Her brother."

Her eyebrows twitched upward, then she gave a nod and picked up her chocolate truffle. I remembered that Julio had said Tony once dated his sister. Since it was at Anna's wedding that I'd discovered Julio, I had assumed that she hadn't clicked with Tony, but she'd apparently at least met his family. Probably she'd been more comfortable with them than I was, so far.

I began composing a question about Tony's other sister, who was married and whom I hadn't met, when a sudden blare of music filled the room. The usual quiet, classical music had been preempted by the Andrews Sisters cheerfully warbling "Six Jerks in a Jeep."

The Aragóns all looked at me. "Tony said you have a ghost that likes music," Theresa said.

True, but I didn't think Captain Dusenberry was into swing.

9

ALL THE CONVERSATIONS in the parlor had stopped, arrested by the sudden injection of saxophones and "Beep, beep!" in three-part harmony. I resisted gritting my teeth, and instead smiled at Theresa Aragón.

"Someone must be playing a joke. Please excuse me for a moment." I stood and went out to the hallway, where I encountered Iz, wide-eyed.

"Iz, could you brew some more tea for our party in Jonquil? Thank you."

I stepped past her as she hurried into the main parlor. At the far end of the hall, a tell-tale figure of fluffy white and yellow was dancing. The Bird Woman's party had spilled out of the dining parlor. Two of the others were doing the jitterbug.

As I came up to them, the Bird Woman turned to me with a joyful grin, singing, "Six creeps in a jeep that leaks!"

I stepped into the butler's pantry, where the house stereo lived, and pushed the eject button. Dee, red-faced, came in from the kitchen and leaned close to murmur in my ear.

"I'm sorry. I tried, but I couldn't stop her."

"A police barricade wouldn't stop her," I whispered back. "It's all right."

I placed the Andrews Sisters disc back in its case and returned the displaced Mozart to the carousel, then turned down the volume and set the music playing on random once more. Soothing strains of a Chopin nocturne emerged from the speakers, and I emerged from the pantry.

"I'm sorry, ladies," I said to the women in the hallway. "I'm afraid that music's a bit too—hic—lively."

"Aw, shoot!" said the Bird Woman. "I just thought it was a

perfect theme song for us. There's six of us, and Peggy drove her Jeep!"

"An admirable choice, I agree," I said, handing her the disc. "Just not for the tearoom."

"If you had one of those tea dances it would work."

"We don't really have room for dancing, I'm afraid." I stepped out of Iz's way as she ducked into the pantry with our empty teapot. Behind her I saw Dee, this time carrying a tray of pumpkin fritters.

"Here's Dee with a special treat for you," I said. "It's a preview from our October menu—no—hic—one else has tasted it yet."

A chorus of "Ooo"s was the response, and Dee sailed across the hall with the plate held high. The ladies followed her into the dining parlor like a flock of ducklings. I couldn't resist closing the door behind them, though I managed not to slam it.

Breathing a sigh of relief, I headed back toward the main parlor and my guests. As I passed the Rose alcove, I noticed Loren watching me. I shot him an apologetic smile, then turned my attention to the Aragóns.

"Sorry about that," I said, resuming my seat. "Where were we?"

"We were talking about your chef," Angela said.

"Oh, yes. I met Julio at his sister Anna's wedding. He made the cake for it, and it was so good I asked who had—hic—had baked it. I was just starting to organize the tearoom at the time."

"Are you Catholic?" Theresa demanded.

Splat. There it was, one of the Big Questions. I took a careful breath.

"No, I was raised a Unitarian."

"Hmf."

Iz came in with a fresh pot of tea, and poured all around. She bent close as she filled my cup.

"Julio says should he send some fritters?" she whispered.

I nodded, then took a swallow of tea. If Theresa was going to grill me, I wanted to be fortified.

But she did not grill me. Instead she mused silently on her own thoughts. Dolores, after giving her a sidelong glance, turned to me.

"Is that a Pueblo girl waiting on us?"

"Yes. Isabel Naranjo. She's from Tesuque."

"She has nice manners."

"Thank you. She's a very sweet girl."

All my servers had good manners. All my staff did, for that matter. I expected no less from my employees.

"Do you really have a ghost?" Angela asked.

"Well..."

"Tony says it's just old wiring," said Theresa, picking up her second truffle.

"Yes, I know that's what—hic—he thinks."

"But you think different?" Angela said.

I gave a helpless shrug. "Some of the things that have happened can't be explained by wiring. The piano in the next alcove, for instance," I said, gesturing toward Iris. "It's played music when no one was near the keyboard."

"How do you know?" Dolores asked.

"I was there."

"And did anyone else witness this?"

She was channeling Tony, and not at his most congenial. I felt my blood pressure go up a notch.

"Yes," I said. "My—my friend, Violetta. Hic." Vi was no longer available to testify, but that was beside the point.

"Doesn't it bother you, to be in a house with ghosts?" Angela asked.

I opened my mouth, but closed it again. To say "no" would have felt insincere. Captain Dusenberry didn't bother me, but Daniel Swazo was a different story. If he really was hanging around, as Willow seemed to think.

Speaking of hanging around, there were other spirits who might be haunting the tearoom. Sylvia Carruthers and Maria Garcia had both died *in* the house. And there was Vi, who had worked here for several months before joining the Opera.

I suddenly felt the need to clear the air.

The Aragóns were watching me, waiting. "I've gotten used to it," I said. It sounded feeble even to me.

To my relief, Iz returned at that moment with a plate of pumpkin fritters and another of meringue pots de crème. Meringues again, but from the gleam of anticipation in Theresa's eye, I figured that wouldn't be a problem.

I passed the fritters around first. My guests appeared to enjoy them. Theresa took two right from the start, which I considered a tribute to Julio's talent.

I put a fritter on my plate and nibbled it. It tasted good, which was a comfort. I wished for the hundredth time that Tony had been able to join us.

The matter of the ghosts bothered me. I wondered if Willow did exorcisms, or knew someone who would. That was a Catholic thing, though. And Willow would probably object to anything that might encourage spirits to leave the tearoom.

Maybe just a cleansing—something involving sage smudge, perhaps. Iz had once suggested a sing. I'd have to ask her about it.

I wrenched my thoughts back to my guests. My Miss Manners angel prompted me to say something, ask a question. I reviewed possible topics: Angela's school (done), Dolores's work (done), Tony (done), Theresa. I knew little about her except that she might have lost her house. Not a good memory to raise.

"Your garden is beautiful," Theresa said, gazing out of the window.

"Thank you."

"Did you plant it yourself?"

"The roses and the flower beds, yes. The wisterias were here. So were the lilacs—hic—on the north side of the house."

"Those are lilacs, those tall bushes?" Angela asked.

"Yes. If you come back in May or June, they'll be blooming."

"I love lilacs."

"Do you like to garden?"

Angela gave me a frightened glance, then picked up her

teacup. Dolores reached for another fritter.

"We live in apartments," she said, "so we don't get to garden."

Oh. Oops. Again.

"When I was younger, yes, I liked to spend time in the yard," Dolores added. She and Theresa exchanged a long glance.

"Well, you're welcome to spend time in mine," I said. "Please feel free to visit."

Dolores gave me a thoughtful look. "Thank you."

I picked up the plate of pots de crème. "These are a new item, if you have room for one more sweet. They may be—hic—a little fragile, so be careful."

The Aragóns each took one. Dolores and Angela watched me and picked up their spoons when I raised mine. Theresa simply popped the whole meringue into her mouth. The crunch as she bit down on it filled the silence.

I scooped out a bit of chocolate crème with my spoon. It was bittersweet and melted on the tongue.

"Those are good," said Theresa when she was able to speak again.

I offered her the plate. She took two more.

"Mama!" Dolores protested.

"It's all right," I said, hoping Theresa wasn't diabetic.

Dolores said something pithy in Spanish. Theresa ignored it, consuming a second meringue with enthusiastic crunching.

"They are very good," said Angela, scooping out the last of the chocolate from her cup.

"Careful," I said. "It might break."

She smiled as she put down her empty spoon, then shot me a mischievous glance and bit the cup. It held together, probably because of the custard. I breathed relief.

"Your Julio invented these?" Dolores asked.

"Yes. He's very creative."

"You better give him a raise, or someone will steal him from you."

Julio already made more than anyone else on the staff besides

Kris and me, and his salary was not that much less than mine.

"Good advice," I said.

Crunch. Theresa had dealt with her third meringue pot. As she chewed it, she eyed the ones left on the plate.

Dolores looked from her to me. "This has been very nice. Thank you, Miss Rosings."

"Ellen, please. Call me Ellen."

She gave a regal nod. "Thank you, Ellen. But now I think it's time for us to go."

Angela hastily finished her tea and put down the cup, then stood and went to retrieve Theresa's walker, which was folded up and tucked against the wall.

"Did Tony arrange for payment?" Dolores asked, just a trifle stiffly.

"It's all taken care of," I said. Tony still had the gift card, but it didn't matter. I'd tell him to use it to bring them back, if they wanted to come.

Angela, holding the walker steady while Theresa used it to pull herself to her feet, glanced at me. "It was wonderful. Thank you for inviting us."

"Thank you for com—hic—coming." I couldn't think of anything more clever to say.

I accompanied them slowly out to the hall. Theresa made a bee-line for the gift shop, and Dolores followed her with a resigned expression. Angela hung back for a moment and turned to me.

"I'm glad I got to meet you," she said shyly. "Tony's told us so much about you."

"Really?" I was surprised. Tony wasn't very talkative, from what I'd seen.

Her shy smile widened. "Oh, yes. He had to explain everything he knew about you before Mama would lend him her car, that one time."

The car that talked. I suppressed a shudder.

"Well, I'm glad I got to meet you, too. I hope you'll come to tea again. Some time."

Angela glanced toward the parlor, looking intimidated, but she nodded. "Some time."

An urge to keep hold of this tenuous connection came over me. I took a tearoom business card out of a stand by the door.

"Do you have a pen?" I asked.

Angela dug one out of her purse for me. I wrote my cell number on the back of the card. "I meant it about coming to visit the garden. You're welcome a—hic—any time. Just let me know and I'll make some lemonade."

"Or tea?" Angela said as I handed her the card, and the hint of a smile on her lips reminded me strongly of Tony.

"Or tea."

Her smile softened as she looked at the card. "That's nice of you. Thanks."

"May I have your number?" I asked.

"Sure."

She wrote it on the back of another tearoom card, then tucked her pen back in her purse and followed her family into the gift shop. I tagged along. Nat smiled at us from the podium.

"Did you enjoy your tea?"

"Oh—" Angela glanced at me. "Yes, it was lovely."

"Let me introduce you," I said to her. "Nat, this is Angela Ar—hic—Aragón, Tony's sister. Angela, this is my aunt Natasha Wheeler. She's the one who advised me to open a tearoom."

"Yes, but you did all the work!" said Nat. "It's a pleasure to meet you, Angela."

Angela smiled and shook Nat's hand. Nat leaned toward her and lowered her voice.

"You don't happen to know any mariachis, do you?"

Angela gave her a blank look. "Mariachis?"

"My fiance wants a mariachi group—just a small one, a trio, maybe—at our wedding reception."

"Oh. No, I'm sorry, I don't know any."

"Have you asked Ramon?" I said to Nat.

"No, but that's a good idea. He's a musician. I should have thought of that."

Angela edged toward her grandmother, who stood before a display of bone china with a seventy-five-dollar teacup in one hand. Her grip looked firm, but I didn't blame Angela for being concerned. None of us would be happy if that cup broke.

"Willow stopped by," Nat told me. "She'd like you to call, to touch base about next week."

"Next week?"

"The spirit tours. October."

"Oh! Hic. Yes, of course. I'll call her."

October would start next week. What had happened to September?

A party of three—mother and two teenaged daughters—emerged from Dahlia, and Nat rang up a package of leaf tea for them. Loren Jackson and his sister came in as they were leaving. The Aragóns had moved on to the shelf of tea accessories, and were deep in discussion.

"Nat, do you have a minute to run to the kitchen?" I asked softly. "Pack up a few sweets for me to send home with them. Ask Julio to put in some of those new meringues, if he has any more." I nodded toward the Aragóns.

"Sure thing! Back in a jiffy."

As she left, the Jacksons stepped up to me. I smiled.

"I hope you enjoyed your tea."

"Oh, yes!" said Shelly, eyes bright with pleasure. "Everything was wonderful."

"Even the...interlude," added Loren. His smile was slight, but it had a dimple to one side, and his eyes were full of laughter.

"Sorry about that," I said, feeling my cheeks redden. "One of our guests got a little carried away."

"Not to worry," he said. "Shelly was wondering if she could buy some of that Wisteria White."

"Yes, it's right over here." Grateful for the change of subject, I led them to the tea shelf.

Dee came in and went to the register. Dolores went up to her and held out one of the leaf-shaped tea strainers. I doubted she was in the habit of brewing tea at home from anything other than tea bags, so it was either a gift for a friend, or a gesture of thanks for my hospitality. Dolores had a strong sense of honor, I concluded.

I stepped out into the hall to give them all more room. I'd have to ask Kris if she'd finished that evaluation of Hyacinth and Poppy versus more room in the gift shop.

"Here you are," Nat said, coming up to me with a white pastry box sealed with our one of our wisteria stickers.

"Thanks." I waited until the Aragóns came out of the gift shop, then pressed the box into Dolores's hands. "For you to enjoy at home. Thank you again for coming. It was lovely to meet you all."

"It was good to meet you," Dolores said, nodding. She squared her shoulders and held her head high. She'd have made a great queen.

I held the front door for them and stood on the *portal* watching them make their way down the path to the car parked at the curb. It was the car that talked—I recognized it. An older model sedan in a sinister shade of dark green.

That had not been a happy evening for me and Tony. With a sigh, I went back in, still wishing he'd been able to join us.

"Beep, beep!"

I jumped, then hiccuped. The Bird Woman grinned at me, shaking out her shawl like a bird fluffing its feathers.

"See you next week for the tour!" she said. "Come on, girls. Beep, beep!"

I did not roll my eyes. I did close them, briefly. When I opened them, the Bird Woman was gone and Dee stood before me.

"Sorry, Ellen," she said.

"Stop apologizing. There's nothing you can do about her."

"She did buy four fifty-dollar gift cards."

I'd never be rid of her. She was my albatross. So to speak.

I put on a smile and said, "That's great. Thanks, Dee."

She smiled back and darted into the gift shop, passing Loren and his sister in the doorway. By Loren's grin, I deduced that they'd witnessed my encounter with the Bird Woman.

"Let me guess," he said. "She's a regular."

I tried not to grimace. "One of our best customers."

"I gather she was responsible for the Andrews Sisters?"

"Yes."

"You'll have to tell me about her. Maybe on Monday?"

"Monday." My brain was becoming a sieve, but I had a vague recollection that I'd made an appointment with him. "Yes," I said, smiling.

"See you then."

After watching the Jacksons out, I wanted nothing more than to go upstairs and collapse. There was one more party in the gift shop, but Dee was handling them. One couple left in the main parlor, in Lily. The day was winding down, none too soon for me.

Nat came up the hall to me. "Poor dear. You look wrung out. Do you want some tea?"

"I've had plenty of tea, thanks. What I need is some alone-time."

And a bubble bath.

And brandy.

Nat patted my arm. "Go on up, sweetie. I'll handle closing."

"You're a love. Thank you."

"You know, you don't have to come over tomorrow."

October was looming. "Yes, I do. We need to fi—hic—nish your dress. We haven't even started mine."

"There's time. Sleep in, if you like. Come for lunch, and we'll work afterward."

"I might not be able to sleep that long."

"You will if you take one of those pills."

"You mean a whole one? I'd sleep 'til Tuesday."

I gave her a hug and a smooch on the cheek, then went upstairs, pausing at the pantry to thank Iz for taking such good care of me and the Aragóns. I passed along Dolores's praise of her manners, which made her blush.

Julio and Ramon were gone for the day. So was Kris. When I stepped onto the upper floor, it was blissfully quiet. Late afternoon light streamed in the western window, softened by the sheers, warming the space. A quiet hush filled the hallway.

Just me and the ghosts.

My shoulders drooped. I really ought to call Willow. I didn't want to.

Better to get it done, I told myself, and went into my office. I turned on all the stained glass lights, which lifted my spirits a little.

A small stack of lavender message slips lay on my desk. I set them aside, resolving not to look at them until Tuesday. Or at least Monday. After lunch.

I couldn't resist looking at my phone to see if Tony had left a text. He had, midday. It was short.

Break on case. Cant do tea. Sorry.

He hadn't had time for more, but at least he'd called his family. Angela, probably. I wondered if she'd had to drop everything and scramble into her pretty clothes.

I looked at the card with Angela's number. Her handwriting was neat, very feminine. I put it in my top drawer.

I liked her, and was glad I'd met her. She wouldn't have come if Tony hadn't had to bail.

I was tempted to answer him, to wish him luck and let him know we'd been fine (well, sort of) without him, but I figured that would just distract him from his work. I'd try in the morning, I decided.

Now, for Willow. Time to get it over with. I called her number and she answered on the third ring.

"Sorry I wasn't available when you stopped by," I said.

"That's all right. I wanted to give you the tour numbers for next week. When's the cutoff for the final total?"

"The day before, please."

I brought up the reservations screen and updated the numbers Willow gave me. More than a week away, and the tours were already filling up. This would definitely be good for the tearoom.

"Thank you for forwarding that report on the knife," Willow said. "I'm afraid I couldn't understand much of it."

"Neither could I. There's meth, though, and something that might be food."

"The meth is puzzling. I don't get a sense that Daniel was a drug user."

"He didn't seem like the type, to me."

"Have you had any more dreams?"

I sighed. "If I did, I don't remember them. I haven't been sleeping all that w—hic—well."

What sleep I'd had was thanks to Nat's pills, but I still tired easily, as though the sleep hadn't been completely restful.

"I do think Daniel wants to communicate with you," Willow said. "How would you feel about my coming over to see if we can reach him?"

"You mean a séance?" I couldn't help recoiling at the thought.

"There's a lot of baggage tied to that word. I just mean the two of us could sit quietly for a while, focus our thoughts, and see if Daniel reaches out to us."

I rubbed my forehead. "Not tonight. It's been a long day and I'm beat."

"Tomorrow?"

"I'm spending the day with my aunt. Maybe in the—hic—evening."

"Shall we touch base mid-afternoon, then?"

"All right. Let me give you my cell number."

When we said goodbye, I put my head in my hands. I really didn't want to commune with Daniel, but I also didn't want to offend Willow right as we were starting this new joint venture.

Was I a wuss for not just saying no? Maybe.

Two light taps startled me into looking up. Nat stood in the doorway, holding the bank bag.

"We're closed," she said. "Mick's finishing up the dishes, and Dee's tidying the parlors. The others have gone home."

I got out my keys and locked the bank bag in Kris's desk.

"Thanks, Nat. See you tomorrow."

She kissed my cheek. "Rest up. If you decide not to come over, just give me a call."

"No, I'm coming. I need to get out."

"Well, go to your inner sanctum and have a drink or something. I'll lock up."

She smiled, hugged me, and nudged me toward my suite. I listened to her footsteps going downstairs, then went into my rooms and firmly closed the door.

I should eat. I'd had too much tea and not enough protein. I opened the fridge, looking for leftovers, but there was only yogurt, lettuce, apples and a few salad veggies. I thought of Gina's lasagna, but it was downstairs in the freezer. Too much trouble, if it was even still there. For all I knew, the staff had had it for lunch.

I wasn't really hungry anyway. Only a little lightheaded.

Maybe a bath? But that seemed like too much trouble as well. Really I just wanted to sit still.

I poured a glass of port—all I had upstairs in the liquor department, besides bottles of wine. There was brandy downstairs in the kitchen, and other exotic liqueurs that Julio used for his magic, but this was easier.

I sat in my favorite chair and took a sip. It wasn't really what I wanted.

I wasn't sure *what* I wanted.

Picking up my book, I tried to settle in to read, but my attention wandered and I found myself starting the same paragraph over and over again. Finally I put the book down and closed my eyes.

I woke to wind rattling the leaves of the trees outside the window. It was dark, and my neck was stiff. I got out of the chair and stumbled to the bathroom, squinting at the clock on my microwave on my way through the kitchenette.

Nine-thirty. Too late to start anything and a little early to crash, but heaven knew I needed the rest. I didn't want to sleep late; I wanted to stop by the flea market in the morning before going to Nat's. There would be an emotional hole there, shaped like Daniel Swazo. Maybe going back would help me remember some little detail of my non-conversation with him.

Or maybe I just wanted to lay the ghost.

I took a sliver of sleeping pill—a little less than a quarter—made a few swipes at my teeth with the toothbrush, and went to bed. As I lay waiting to fall asleep, I thought over my tea with the Aragóns.

It had not been too awful, really, except for my suffering from a strong case of foot-in-mouth disease. Theresa had enjoyed the sweets, and Angela seemed sympathetic. I hadn't learned much about Dolores, except that she still grieved for her husband and she shared Tony's pride.

They all did, in varying degrees. Maybe I'd never get past it.

I wondered if it would have been different with Tony there. Would Dolores have followed his lead and tried to like me? Would he have been able to cajole Theresa? Or would it have been even worse?

My thoughts drifted from these futile speculations to my upcoming obligations. Finishing Nat's dress was top priority, followed by making mine. Then I'd need to meet with Julio and Nat about the menu for the wedding, get an update on how many guests there would be and decide about the shade—tent or umbrellas. Order champagne.

From that, I progressed to pouring champagne. Bottle after bottle for an endless stream of thirsty guests. The Bird Woman came by with two pilsner glasses, demanding to have them filled, which took most of a bottle. She sallied off and climbed into a jeep without spilling a drop while I reached for another bottle to open.

I couldn't get the foil off, so I looked for my corkscrew to get it started. Instead I found a knife on the table in front of me. A knife with a handle of turquoise, malachite, and sugilite.

I looked up and saw Daniel Swazo staring at me.

He was dressed all in white, but not like Zozobra. Around his hips was knotted a sash of red, white, and black. It looked like a ceremonial garment.

Behind him, the line of people waiting for champagne was getting restless.

"I don't know what to do," I told him.

He pointed to the knife. I didn't want to touch it. It wasn't mine; it wasn't my responsibility.

"Beep, beep!" said someone in line. Others took up the call, until the whole line was beeping at me, holding out empty champagne flutes.

Daniel stood silent, staring intently at me, pointing at the knife.

I had to get the champagne open, and this was the only way. I picked up the knife.

A terrible sense of wrongness filled me. Not the knife itself, not Daniel, but something was wrong, very wrong, and it would hurt the family; it would hurt the tribe. I had to do something, tell someone, but it was hard to walk, hard to breathe, and the hill was steep. Night would come soon. I had to get help. I had to let someone know.

Then I fell, endlessly, into darkness.

10

THAT TIME, I was sure I screamed.

I woke, struggling with my sheets until I realized they weren't attacking me. I was home, in bed, not falling.

I collapsed and wept helplessly, great wracking sobs, punctuated by hiccups. Finally I dragged myself up and turned on the light.

"Damn you, Daniel!" I gasped.

That wasn't fair, I knew. Daniel had died. Someone had beaten him and it killed him, whether or not that was the intent. He'd done nothing wrong that I knew of. He deserved my pity, and if I could give it, my help.

A gust of wind slapped the window. I got up and went to my sitting room, turning on lights. My half-drunk port sat on the table by my chair. I downed it in two gulps.

As I carried the empty glass into the kitchenette, I thought about refilling it. But I didn't need more port. I needed rest. I needed peace.

I put the glass in the sink and leaned my hands on the edge of the counter. A particularly painful hiccup set my tears flowing again. My gaze fell on the handle of the cutlery drawer beside me.

There were knives in there—sharp ones. It would be so easy to take one out. A simple matter to open my flesh and let the blood flow. The bathtub was two steps away; it needn't make a mess.

"No," I said aloud, my voice dulled by tears. "I'm stronger than that."

It wasn't the first time I'd had such thoughts. After my father's death, I'd lived in a black hole of depression for a while.

I'd learned ways to fight the darkness.

I left the knives where they were and went into the bathroom, stripping off my nightclothes and dropping them on the floor. I got in the shower and ran hot water on my head for a long time. When my fingers started to wrinkle, I rubbed some shampoo into my hair and scratched my scalp thoroughly.

I toweled off and dressed in clean sweats, then decided I'd better eat. I still wasn't hungry, but that wasn't a good sign. Lettuce and yogurt wouldn't cut it. I needed Gina's lasagna.

I left my suite and crossed the upper hall toward the light switches. The chandelier came on before I got there.

I stopped, heart suddenly racing. There was no one else there; I strained my ears but heard only the wind. I turned in a slow circle, seeing nothing unusual, then started toward the stairs.

The stairwell lights came on. I swallowed, then continued.

The downstairs hall light was on by the time I reached the foot of the stairs. The pantry light came on as I turned toward it, and the kitchen lights came on as I entered the kitchen. Behind me, the stereo began playing soft music.

I paused. "Thank you, Captain."

I went to the big, industrial freezer where I'd stashed the lasagna. It was still there, with a note in Julio's handwriting taped to it: "Ellen's – hands off."

My eyes fugged up with tears. Julio had guarded my lasagna. People loved me.

The pan was huge, a square casserole that would feed half a dozen. Frozen hard. I turned on the smaller of the two ovens and put the whole pan in, not caring to try to carve out a single serving.

While I waited, I decided to eat dessert first. I raided the fridge for two leftover petit fours and a chicken curry tea sandwich. I sat at the break table to eat them, listening to the occasional ticking from the oven as various bits of metal heated up.

The curry made me thirsty, so I poured myself a glass of

water. I felt better for the food, but it wasn't enough. I was hungry now, and the lasagna would take a while. I could walk through the tearoom while I waited....

Do it, I told my reluctant self. The only ghost around is the friendly one.

I took my water with me. My slippers shuffled on the hardwood floor of the hall. Lights came on ahead of me. It was like one of those futuristic homes where everything was computer driven, or the frozen food aisle in the supermarket, where the ice cream cases had motion-sensitive lights that flickered to life to entice the passer-by.

The captain had figured out some new tricks. He'd never messed with the upstairs lights before, or the main parlor and the gift shop, yet both were illuminated as I stepped in and looked at each of the alcoves.

Everything was in order. The tables were clean, every stray crumb had been vacuumed, all was ready for Tuesday morning.

I stood in Violet, looking up at Vi's portrait. Such a lovely smile. I didn't think she was here, hanging around the tearoom. She'd never been one to dawdle when she had better things to do.

A feeling of peace settled over me. I loved this little room, the most remote corner of the public area. I sat in one of the wing chairs and gazed at the décor that Nat and the servers had helped me with. Every piece of furniture, every fabric, every touch of art, had been carefully chosen. More than any of the other alcoves, though I loved all of them, this space was personally meaningful to me.

I hadn't shown it to Vi's mother yet, but I felt it would soon be time. Maybe in December, when she'd be missing her daughter during the holiday season. I made a mental note to ask in a few weeks.

An aroma of garlic and tomato was beginning to drift through the tearoom; most uncharacteristic. I returned to the kitchen to find the lasagna happily bubbling away. I fixed myself a plate and turned to the break table, then changed my mind.

Captain Dusenberry was being very kind. I would have my midnight supper in his room.

I collected a place mat along with some silverware and carried everything across the hall to the dining parlor. The chandelier came on as I reached the doorway. I set my place at the center of the table's west side, so I could look out the French doors. When I pushed aside the sheers, I saw moonlight pooled outside and the branches of the lilacs waving in the wind.

The first bite of lasagna made me sigh with bliss. Gina always made it the way her grandmother did: spinach and mushrooms, no meat, and lots of garlic. I was pretty sure she also made her own marinara sauce. She wasn't ordinarily opposed to shortcuts, but this was Nonna Fiorello's recipe.

As I ate, I thought about Captain Dusenberry. I was sure the Navy revolver was the key to figuring out who had killed him. I knew from the contemporary newspaper stories that a ball had been dug out of the wall of this room, but it had apparently not ended up in the Museum's collection.

What if there was another ball still in the wall?

A shiver went through me. Two bullets had struck Captain Dusenberry. Had they both ended up in the wall?

I needed a metal detector. Maybe Tony would be able to get his hands on one—except Tony was busy with his case.

The reenactor. Mr. Quentin. Those guys sometimes used metal detectors, going over battlefields looking for artifacts. I'd talk to him. Maybe he could bring a detector over and we could go over the walls.

Excitement made me want to jump up and contact him that minute, but it was the middle of the freaking night. All I had was his phone number; I wasn't even sure he had email. I'd have to wait until a more civilized hour.

I finished my lasagna and drank my water, thinking about what would happen if I did find a bullet in the wall. A ballistics test—would that cost money? Probably. And what would I compare it to? I'd have to find a candidate for the gun, one that had belonged to one of the Hidalgos, and have that tested, too.

This could get expensive.

Maybe the Museum would pay for part of the testing? If the results could be used for an article? Bennett Cole could write something; the history buffs would love it. Hundred-fifty-year-old murder solved!

Or maybe I was the only one who cared.

I sighed, glancing up at the chandelier. One crystal, in the exact center of the side nearest me, was swinging gently back and forth.

"I'll do it," I said, smiling. "I'll find a—hic—way."

My water glass was empty, and my full stomach was making me drowsy. That was good—drowsy was good. I carried my dishes to the kitchen and washed them, because I didn't want to be a total pig. Put away the lasagna, tidied the kitchen, then refilled my glass and carried it upstairs, turning out the kitchen light as I passed the switch.

When I stepped into the hall, the parlor lights were out, and the pantry light turned off behind me. The music stayed on, though: Mozart, I thought. I left it.

When I reached the upper floor, the stairwell lights went out. I stepped to the switches and turned off the chandelier.

"Thank you, Captain," I said again, and crossed the darkened hall to my suite, where the lights were still burning. Here, in my private space, he left the lights to me. I shut them off in the main room and returned to my bedroom, where I made a ceremony of straightening the bedclothes and fluffing the pillows.

"Daniel," I said, with an absolutely straight face, "I have not forgotten about the knife. I'm going to follow up on it tomorrow. Please let me get a good night's sleep."

I took one last swallow of water, set the glass on my nightstand, and climbed into bed.

I slept well, undisturbed by further dreams. Apparently Daniel felt he'd gotten his message across. Maybe the day would bring me further understanding.

The hiccups were still with me when I woke, which was disappointing, but at least I no longer felt deeply depressed. I got up and dressed, ate some yogurt and an apple for breakfast, and hopped in my car to head for the flea market.

The sky was brilliant blue, with a scattering of pillowy clouds that might get serious later in the day. I smelled frybread on the breeze as I crossed the parking lot, and contemplated a second breakfast.

Nat would feed me well, though. I resisted, bypassing the food stands and making my way back to the Tesuque artists' tent.

The jewelers and the doll-maker were there. The man selling bread was at the end of the row, and I was surprised to see a table covered with stone-inlaid knives next to his. On first seeing them, I shivered. I picked up a doll from the neighboring table to buy myself some breathing time.

The doll's dress was red velvet, like Nat's wedding dress. I made a show of examining the details, while the doll-maker watched me placidly.

I saw movement to my right and glanced that way. An older Pueblo woman—petite, with strands of silver in her dark hair—had come up to the table of knives and stood adjusting them as they lay on the cotton tablecloth. She was bundled in a shawl despite the mild day, and she looked sad.

Daniel's mother. Or grandmother? I drew a sharp breath.

She shouldn't be here, not so soon, not while her grief was still fresh. She touched each knife tenderly, as if remembering their maker.

Maybe she needed to sell them, to let them go. Or maybe she needed the money.

I looked at the doll-maker. "I'll take this one." I'd give it to Nat, as a pre-wedding gift. She didn't want a shower, but she'd agreed to a tea with a few friends to celebrate her engagement.

While the artist was putting the doll in a recycled grocery bag for me, I turned to the knife table. "Those are very pretty. I was admiring them last—hic—week."

The woman looked up at me with woe-weary eyes and a

shadow of a smile. "Thank you. My son's work."

Her voice was a little rough. Probably she'd been crying a lot.

There were fewer knives than last week. I looked at each of them, again debating whether to buy one for Manny. It would be a gift to Daniel's mother as well, and that made me more inclined.

A folded pocket knife caught my eye. It had broad bands of turquoise and narrower stripes of something pale green, either a different turquoise or jade.

I reached toward it, then hesitated. In the dream, touching Daniel's knife had not been a good idea.

This was not a dream, however, and this was not Daniel's personal knife, even though he had made it. I steeled myself to run a finger along the stone inlay. It was perfectly smooth; I couldn't feel a seam anywhere. Beautiful work.

The back of my neck tingled. I glanced up at the man with the bread. He was watching me. For a second his face reminded me of Daniel's, except for a tightness to the skin around his eyes. Was it Daniel's brother, then? He was taller, more muscular. Belatedly, he smiled, but his eyes were still watchful.

"Tomás," Daniel's mother said to him, and then followed with something in Tewa. So it was Daniel's brother; Tommy, the detective had called him.

Mrs. Swazo stepped over to arrange the loaves of bread more neatly. I followed.

"Did you bake—hic—the bread?" I asked her.

"Yes. This morning."

"It's beautiful." I picked up a loaf that was a cluster of lumps, like pull-apart rolls except in a flower shape rather than a rectangle. "I'll take this one, and this knife."

I pointed to the pocket knife. While Mrs. Swazo bustled about getting me a bag, I collected my doll from the doll-maker. I'd have to stop by an ATM to replenish my pocket money, I thought ruefully, but I didn't regret these purchases.

A young Hispanic man with a shaved head and tattoos climbing up his neck came up to Daniel's brother, who shook his head and muttered, "Not today." Tommy's gaze shot to Mrs. Swazo, then to me. I looked away.

I didn't like him. Iz's words came back to me—something about him always being in trouble. I looked at his mother, wondering how much grief he had caused her.

"Here you go," she said with a brave smile, handing me the bag. I paid her and thanked her, then strolled down the aisle. I wanted to get away from Tommy; I didn't like his eyes. It was good that he was helping his mother, but I wouldn't mind never seeing him again.

I walked out to the parking lot, feeling sad for Daniel's mom. I would have liked to help her more, but she probably didn't come to the flea market every week. She hadn't been there the previous week; it had just been Daniel and Tommy.

Giving myself a shake, I let go of thinking about Tommy Swazo, and turned my thoughts to my own family instead. I put my gifts for Nat and Manny in the trunk of my car, and took the bread with me in the front. I'd give it to Nat, who would probably feed it to me with lunch, which I wouldn't mind. Yes, it was sinful bread, but it smelled so good...

Sinful bread. Something niggled at me on those words. I put my keys in the ignition but didn't start the car, trying to pin down the thought.

My phone buzzed. I took it out and saw that it was a text from Tony.

> Sorry about yesterday. Might get some time free today. Want to do a movie?

Aargh. My day was spoken for, but I didn't want to put Tony off again. I typed a quick answer:

> Working on Nat's wedding dress. What about tonight?

He didn't reply immediately. I started the car and headed for Nat's house. The phone buzzed while I was driving, but I waited until I was parked in the driveway before checking it.

Let me check. Get back soon.

I slipped the phone in my pocket so I'd be sure to catch Tony's text, then grabbed the bread and got out. Manny was on the *portal* scrubbing the grill. He looked up at me with a grin.

"I found a mariachi band! My cousin Tabo knows a guy who's in one."

I quaked in my shoes, but bravely asked him, "How many trumpets?"

"None. Just two guitars, a violin, a *vihuela* and a *guitarrón*."

"Is the *guitarrón* the big thing that looks like a cross between a guitar and a string bass?"

"Yeah, and the *vihuela* is the little baby guitar."

"Is there a singer?"

"They all sing. They're really good—I went and listened to them the other night. It'll be great!"

I smiled. "Congratulations! That's one chore off the list."

He laughed. "Yeah. Now for the other hundred and fifty!"

I kissed his cheek and went inside. Nat was at the stove, peering into a stew pot.

"I brought bread," I said, setting it on the counter next to her.

"You've been to the flea market!" She picked up the loaf and held it to her face, inhaling deeply. "Ahh. I was really tempted by these last time."

"Me, too. I caved today."

She put the bread down and reached for a spoon to stir the pot. "It'll go great with this."

"What's 'this'? I smell garlic." I leaned against her, peering into the pot, where I saw chunks of chicken, tomato, and green pepper.

"It's 'clean the fridge' soup."

"Works for me."

Nat laid the spoon on a ceramic sunflower on the counter and put a lid on the pot, trapping all the yummy smells inside. "Shall we get started? Maybe we can finish my dress by lunch, and move on to yours."

We did that, with the help of tea and oranges. Right before

noon, Nat tried on her dress and stood in front of the full-length mirror in her bedroom while I plucked at the hems and snipped off stray threads.

"Oh, Ellen. It's beautiful. Just what I've wanted all these years!"

I met her gaze in the mirror and couldn't help smiling. The burgundy velvet gleamed softly in the muted light from the window, its richly-gathered, tiered skirt a plush waterfall. Nat's favorite concho belt caught the blouse to her waist in flattering folds. Above the pointed collar, set off nicely by the silver buttons, Nat's face beamed with happiness, and that made me happy, too.

Despite the strands of silver in her dark curls, she was still beautiful. My beloved aunt, my last connection with my parents' generation. I gave her a big hug.

"So, do I get lunch now? I'm starving."

"Yes, yes! Let me take this off."

When we got to the kitchen, we found Manny peering into the soup pot. He looked up like a kid caught stalking the cookie jar.

"Just making sure it wasn't burning." He put the lid back on. "Hey, want to hear Los Gatos? I got their CD."

"Sure," Nat said, smiling as she took down plates and bowls from the cupboard.

I grabbed a plate for the bread and fetched Nat's butter keeper from the back of the counter, then brought them to the kitchenette table, where a handful of sunflowers stood in a stubby green ceramic vase. Manny plugged his CD into Nat's ancient boom box on the counter, and mariachi music filled the room. The first piece started slowly, march-like, but then quickly accelerated into boisterous waltz-time.

"I know that one!" I said. "What's it called?"

"La Negra," Manny said. "It's kind of the mariachi national anthem."

I nodded, swaying to the music. Manny caught me in his arms and danced me around the room.

"Careful!" Nat said, dodging us as she set the table.

We narrowly avoided crashing into a plant stand and separated, laughing. I hiccuped. Manny went to the fridge, looking for beer.

"May I help serve?" I asked Nat.

"No, I've got it," she said. "Go ahead and sit down."

I took a moment to check my phone and found a text from Tony:

Not sure what time I can get off

I typed back:

Just come to Nat's when you're free.

After a moment he answered, "OK." I put my phone away and hurried to the table.

"This smells fantastic," I said over the music.

Nat smiled. "Thank you. Manny, could you turn that down a smidge?"

Manny got up and danced over to the counter to obey. "But they're good, aren't they? You like them?"

"They sound wonderful. I'm sure they'll be perfect."

I smiled and dug into my soup. The mariachis didn't sound *too* raucous. The lack of trumpets was reassuring. More important, Manny's beaming face and Nat's fond glances at him made me feel that the wedding would be a success.

"Joe's coming for the wedding," Nat said to me. "Did he tell you?"

"I haven't heard from him, no. It'll be good to see him."

Privately, I was a little miffed that my brother hadn't told me he'd be at Nat's wedding, but it was true that we didn't communicate much. He had his own world, and I had mine, and there wasn't much in common between them.

"Thank you for bringing this bread, Ellen," Nat said as she tore a bun from the flower.

I did likewise, popping a bit of bread into my mouth and

closing my eyes as I savored its sinful deliciousness, the guilty pleasure of carbohydrates with little or no nutritional value.

Sinful bread. That niggling thought was back. I watched Manny pull off a chunk for himself, tear it in half, and lavish it with soft butter.

Could the food on Daniel's knife be bread?

A cold tingle washed down my arms, accompanied by a vision of Daniel stabbing a loaf of his mother's bread.

And then dipping the knife in meth? It made no sense.

Why would he stab the bread? Why use a knife when the bread was meant to be pulled apart?

"Wool-gathering, Ellen?" asked Nat.

"Sorry. Distracted."

I returned my attention to the soup, and listened to Nat and Manny talk about the wedding. Now that the music was lined up, most of the planning was done, and they were down to choosing what they wanted on the menu.

My thoughts drifted. How could bread *and* meth have gotten on Daniel's knife? I wanted to ask Tony, or at least pass along my thought to him. But it wasn't his case.

I could call Detective Walters, but what would I say to him? How would I explain that I knew about the lab test? He'd be angry.

I had to let Tony get the information to him. Or maybe suggest that Tony talk to the lab techs and determine whether the food on the knife really was bread.

My instinct was that this was important, but I felt that I didn't completely understand why. I kept puzzling at it while I finished my lunch.

When her bowl was empty, Nat stood, picking up her plate and Manny's. "Well, shall we get back to work?"

"Yes, let's." I ate the last of my bread, resisting the temptation to grab another piece, and carried my dishes to the sink.

"If we get a good start on your dress today, maybe we can finish it tomorrow," Nat added.

I nodded, still chewing.

"You mean yours is done?" Manny said. "I want to see it!"

Nat gave him a coy smile. "Not until the wedding."

He continued to pester her about it, playfully. She bantered with him in the best of cheer, and didn't yield an inch. Finally he hugged us both and grabbed his denim jacket from a hook by the door.

"I'm going to the hardware store. Need anything?"

"No, thanks," Nat said. "Be back by six if you want dinner."

"Yes, ma'am!" He kissed her cheek and headed out the door, whistling mariachi music.

I checked my phone again, but there was no message. Nat gave me an amused look.

"Expecting a call?"

"Tony and I might go to a movie to—hic—tonight, but he's not sure when he'll be free. He'll probably come by here."

"Ah."

We cut out the pieces for my dress, and I started to feel excited about it. Like Nat, I had admired these dresses all my life, and secretly longed to own one. Just handling the fabric was a sensory delight; the sapphire velvet was luxuriously soft and lustrous.

Nat started putting the skirt together while I worked on the tunic. With hands busy, my mind was free to wander, and I wound up picking at the problem of Daniel Swazo's knife once more.

Why would there be bread on the knife? Assuming, for the moment, that the stuff on the knife was, in fact, bread.

I thought about Mrs. Swazo's breads, all the wonderful shapes she made. I remembered looking at them a week before, the morning Nat and I had gone looking for buttons. A scene clicked into my memory from that morning: the knotwork bread I'd admired.

That was the last one. Sorry.

Tommy Swazo had refused to sell me that loaf, but he'd sold it to the young man in jeans.

Then this morning, another young man with a tattooed neck

had approached Tommy's table.

Not today.

I thought about the breads that had been on the table that morning. I hadn't paid close attention; I'd been more focused on Mrs. Swazo and her grief. But I was pretty sure that there hadn't been any of the knotwork loaves there today.

Nor, in fact, had there been any on the table the previous week. Tommy had taken the loaf out from beneath the table when the man in jeans came up to him.

That was the last one.

I drew a long, deep breath.

What if the meth was in the bread?

My mouth went dry. Maybe Daniel had noticed the exchange. Maybe he'd found a moment to examine the loaves under the table. Maybe he'd slid his knife into one to confirm his suspicions.

It was all supposition, but it fit. It fit better than anything else I could think of.

Daniel Swazo had died as a result of being beaten. Had he confronted Tommy, leading to a fight?

I had to talk to Tony.

I finished a seam and set aside the blouse, then reached for my phone. Nat glanced up at me, then went back to work gathering a tier of the skirt. I sent a hasty text to Tony.

Idea about knife. Need to talk.

My nerves were buzzing with the urge to *do* something, so I stood and picked up my mug. "Want some more coffee?"

"Sure," Nat said, holding out her mug. "Cream and one spoon of sugar."

In the kitchen, afternoon shadows had already fallen, making the room seem chilly. I fixed our coffees and was turning to go back when something about the window caught my attention. I paused to look, and froze as I realized a man stood outside on the *portal*, looking in.

Tommy Swazo.

11

I STIFLED A STARTLED YELP. Coffee splashed across my hand.

Swazo stared at me for an eternal second, during which I could not help thinking about those powerful arms raised in anger, those big fists thumping down on a surprised, smaller brother. He smiled—not a friendly smile—and stepped to one side, out of view, releasing me from paralysis.

I put the mugs on the table and ran to the door to make sure it was locked. As I confirmed it, a thump fell against the heavy wood; it shook against my hands.

Heart pounding, I peeked through the small, barred window high in the door. Swazo was striding away down the driveway.

"Ellen?" Nat called from the living room. "Are you all right?"

"Are all the doors locked?" I called back. "I'm OK, but there's a man outside."

Nat's footsteps hurried toward the kitchen. I grabbed a dish towel and dried my hands, trying not to shake.

"Did he ring the doorbell?" Nat said as she joined me, frowning in concern.

I shook my head. "I think he's gone now. He w—hic—was standing outside the window, and when he saw me he left."

"Oh, Ellen!"

"I think it was Daniel Swazo's brother. He banged on the door and then went down the driveway."

"I'm calling the police," she said, reaching for the phone.

"Not 911. It's not—hic—not an emergency."

"He was trespassing!"

"But he's gone now. Let me call...I'd better call Detective Walters."

I would much rather have called Tony, but it wasn't his case.

Walters would want to know about Swazo's trespassing.

Nat offered me the phone, but I shook my head. "I don't know his number. It's on my cell."

"I have it here." She took a business card from her bulletin board and handed it to me.

My throat was dry. I took a swig of my coffee and tried to gather my thoughts.

I shouldn't mention the knife or what was on it. I was tempted to nudge Walters toward thinking about it, but that could be disastrous. I had to talk to Tony and let him be the one to raise the subject.

OK. No knife. Just tell him Swazo was here.

I swallowed some more coffee, then dialed Walters's number. It went to voicemail. I left a brief message telling him about Swazo, mentioning that I'd seen him that morning at the flea market and leaving Nat's number. I only hiccuped twice.

As I hung up the phone, Nat gathered me into a hug. "You look like you've seen a ghost."

I laughed. "I like ghosts better."

"You're trembling. Come and sit down."

We sat at the table and drank coffee. Gradually the tension in my shoulders relaxed. Outside, late afternoon shadows crept across the hillside and lengthened beneath the piñons.

"He must have followed me here from the flea—hic—market," I said. The thought made me unhappy; I'd been so adamant that Daniel had not followed us, and now his brother appeared to have done so. It weakened my position. I could imagine Detective Walters saying, "I told you so."

I wondered if Swazo had left any footprints on the *portal*. If he had, and if the police had found any footprints the day Daniel died, maybe they could match them. It was a long shot, but I got up to check.

Nat followed me to the door. "Ellen?"

"I'm just going to look at something."

If there were prints, I didn't want Manny to walk across them when he got back. I unlocked the door and opened it.

"Oh!"

Stuck into the door's center panel, right below the window, was a knife. Its handle was beautifully inlaid with stripes of turquoise and coral. One of Daniel's.

Behind me, Nat let out a gasp.

"Don't touch it," I said. "Do you have a plastic bag?"

"I'll get one." Nat stepped away and I heard her pull open a drawer.

The knife looked familiar. It might have been on Mrs. Swazo's table at the market that morning. Tommy must have helped himself.

I swallowed, the implied threat sinking in. He was telling me to back off.

"Is this big enough?" Nat asked, holding out a food storage bag.

I took it, wondering how to remove the knife without damaging any prints that might be on it. Maybe I could slide the bag over it, and pull on the blade...

The sound of a motorcycle drew my attention to the street. A bike came down the hill and turned into the driveway.

"Tony." I exhaled relief. "Let's wait. He'll know what to do."

Tony parked by my car and swung off the bike, removing his helmet, which ruffled his short, dark hair. I caught my breath, struck anew by his good looks.

His smile faded as he came up to the doorway and saw the knife. "What's this?"

"A warning," I said. "Tommy Swazo was just here."

"Swazo?" He frowned. "That's..."

"The brother of the man I found la—hic—last week. We were about to put it in this." I offered him the storage bag.

He looked at it, then at me. "You've got the hiccups again?"

"Still."

Tony's expression sharpened with concern, then he sighed. "I'll get an evidence bag. Don't touch it."

Nat gently took the plastic bag from my hands. "I'll make some more coffee."

I watched Tony retrieve a plastic bag with printing on it from one of the saddlebags on his bike. Gina's recommendation that I get laid flashed through my mind, bringing heat to my cheeks. He returned, took several photos of the knife with his phone, then carefully removed the knife from the door.

Tony shot a glance at me as he pulled a marker out of his jacket pocket and wrote on the bag. "Tell me what happened."

I told him, describing Swazo's appearance outside the window and the thump against the door as he departed. "I didn't realize until now that it was a knife. Oh! I was going to check if he left footprints..."

"If he did, they're probably gone by now. Does Walters know about this?"

"I called and got his voicemail. I left him a message."

"Hm."

"Come in and close the door," Nat said. "Tony, would you like some coffee?"

"Yes, but I need to call this in. Just take a sec."

I stepped in and Tony pulled the door closed, remaining outside. I watched through the window as he went back to his bike and locked the knife in the saddlebag, took out his phone and took a couple more photos of the door, then made a call. He paced in the driveway, restless as a caged jaguar. Finally he put the phone away and headed for the door. I opened it for him.

He paused to finger the mark the knife had left, frowning. "Sorry about that."

"You didn't do it. Come on in."

Nat clucked and fussed about settling us at the table with coffee. Tony took a long pull at his mug and then closed his eyes. "Oh, that's good."

"Thank you," Nat said. "Julio shared his source with me."

I took another swig of mine; I hadn't recognized it as Julio's Colombian, but maybe it was a different blend.

"I requested a patrol for your house," Tony told Nat. "They'll come by a couple of times a day, and at night, for the next couple of weeks."

"Thank you," Nat said, then glanced at me. "Are you doing the same for Ellen's house?"

"Swazo doesn't know where I live," I said.

"Want to bet?" Tony said.

I lifted my mug. I didn't like it when he got cynical, and it certainly wasn't any comfort.

"He may know your name, from the police report. He's seen you at the flea market...twice?"

I nodded.

"And he probably knows you're the one who found his brother. Don't go back to the flea market."

"I won't." I thought fleetingly of Mrs. Swazo, feeling a rush of pity for her, but there was nothing I could do for her. Nothing except, perhaps, make sure Tommy got locked up. She might not consider that a favor.

"Tony, I need to talk to you about the knife. Not this one—the one from last week."

"Too many knives around here."

"Yes. Well, I was thinking about that report." I glanced at Nat, then decided she might as well know everything. If I couldn't trust Nat, I couldn't trust anyone.

"That chemical analysis I ask—hic—asked you about a couple of days ago," I said to her. "It was for what was on Daniel Swazo's knife that was found in your driveway."

Nat tilted her head. "The one Dee said was meth?"

"Yes. And she mentioned that the other things in the report sounded like food." With a sidelong glance I saw Tony frowning, but he said nothing. I continued. "Well, I was thinking about it, and I realized it might be bread. You know that bread I brought from the flea market? Daniel Swazo's mother baked it."

"Daniel and Tommy Swazo's mother," Tony said.

"Yes. And the first time we went to the market, she wasn't there. Tommy was selling her bread, and there was one—hic—shape he had under the table. He sold a loaf to a guy who came up, but he wouldn't sell one to me. He said he was out, but I think that wasn't true. There was a box under the table."

Tony's chin rose and his brows drew together. "He's hiding meth in his mother's bread?"

"I think so. I don't have any proof, but it's the only thing that makes sense. And Daniel was selling his knives right near Tommy's table. If he suspected, he might have used his knife to check the bread. And if Tommy noticed..."

"He might have beat the crap out of his brother."

"But why did Daniel follow us here?" Nat asked.

"I don't think he did," I said. "Tommy must have dropped him on the frontage road. Daniel was looking for help, and this was the nearest house. Only he didn't make it to the door."

Nat shook her head. "Poor boy."

I swallowed, turning back to Tony. "There was a man at the market this morning, with tattoos on his neck. Tommy told him 'Not today.' Mrs. Swazo was there, selling off Daniel's knives."

Tony's eyes narrowed. "I'd better call Walters."

"I did try. I didn't mention the report."

"Good. Gonna have to figure out what to say to him. He won't like that I gave it to you."

"Maybe you don't have to tell him that."

"If he asks, I've got to tell him."

"Maybe he won't ask?" The thought that I might get Tony in trouble worried me.

He sat gazing at nothing, frowning slightly. I took advantage of his distraction to appreciate the clean lines of his face. Well, not entirely clean; it looked as if he hadn't shaved in a couple of days. His jaw was tight and there were shadows under his eyes. A small, vertical crease had formed between his dark eyebrows. Apparently, he'd had about as much rest as I had in the past week.

He noticed me watching him and met my gaze. The frown softened.

"Don't worry. If I have to tell Walters that I shared the report with you, it might pi—it might make him mad, but it won't do any harm. You're a consultant, remember?"

I smiled, laughed a little, and hiccuped. Tony put his hand

over mine, sending a tingle shooting up my arm.

"This is helpful, OK? You're doing good stuff, not bad stuff. Don't worry."

His hand was warm. He curled his fingertips into my palm and squeezed.

"I think you nailed this one. Probably he didn't mean to, but I bet Tommy is the one who killed his brother."

I nodded. "There's no proof, though."

"Maybe we just haven't found it yet. If Walters takes a closer look at Tommy, who knows what he'll turn up? Leave it to him, now."

"By all means."

He gave my hand another squeeze, then let go and stood, looking at Nat. "Will you excuse me? I'd better give Walters a call."

"Of course."

We stayed at the table while Tony went outside to make his call. After a moment I realized Nat was watching me, and looked up at her.

"I think his manners are improving." She smiled, the skin around her eyes crinkling with amusement. "More coffee?"

I shook my head. "I'm floating."

"It's time to start dinner anyway."

I got up to help, and Nat assigned me the duty of making red chile sauce for enchiladas. Simple and soothing task, starting with a roux of oil and flour, then adding seasonings and the puréed chile that Nat preferred to using powdered. Its color was vibrant red, and it would be brilliant on the plate.

"I'm sorry about the damage to your door," I said while she pulled veggies, tortillas, and cheese out of the refrigerator. "And for leading Swazo to your h—hic—house. I feel like I've placed you in danger."

"I doubt he'll come back. He made his point."

"So to speak."

Nat chuckled, which made me feel better. She sliced some onions and started them sautéeing, which filled the kitchen with a delicious aroma. Suddenly I was hungry.

Male voices sounded outside the door, then it opened and Manny came in, followed by Tony. Nat greeted her intended with a smooch on the cheek. Manny hugged her, then turned to me.

"Chica, you should spend the night here with your aunt. You shouldn't be alone."

"I gather Tony filled you in on our visitor."

Manny's bushy brows gathered into a frown. "He better not come back, that's all. I'll be in the garage," he added, kissing Nat's cheek before he left.

I looked at Tony, who had stayed near the door. "Did you reach Walters?"

"Yeah. He's on his way over. He'll want to hear it from you. The report didn't come up, but I told him about the bread Swazo wouldn't sell you."

"OK."

"Tony, would you like to stay for dinner?" Nat asked.

"It's Sunday," I said.

"Oh, crap," Tony said, then looked up guiltily at Nat. "Sorry. Um, I need to make a call."

I glanced at Nat's kitchen clock as Tony went back outside. It was quarter to six; he might already be too late.

"What does Sunday matter?" Nat asked.

"He usually eats dinner with his family on Sundays. If he isn't working."

"Oh." Nat began slicing zucchini. "Well, he seems to be working today."

It was nice of Nat to invite him to join us. Other than our evening at the Opera, she hadn't seen him socially at all. She'd made the invitation for my sake, which was kind of her. My cheeks grew warm at the thought that she was welcoming him into the family.

The sauce had thickened nicely. Turning the heat down to low, I set the spoon on the sunflower spoon rest. "What else can I help with?"

Nat put the zucchini into the pan with the onions, then

reached for a yellow squash. "Start the oil heating for the tortillas, then you can set the table if you like."

I pulled out one of Nat's prized cast-iron skillets, poured some oil into it, and turned on the burner. Nat preferred gas stoves to electric, and so did I. Leaving the blue flames caressing the bottom of the skillet, I cleared the coffee mugs off the table and set them on the counter.

Tony came back in, looking a bit lost-puppyish. His hands were shoved in his pockets, shoulders hunched forward.

"Did you reach your mother?" I asked. "Are you going?"

"Nah, I have to wait for Walters. She's annoyed. I missed dinner last week, too."

"Because of your case. I keep forgetting that th—hic—this one isn't. I'm—"

"Don't be sorry."

His abruptness silenced me. I turned to the stove and tested the oil with a drop of water. It sizzled.

"This is hot," I said to Nat.

"Good." She handed me a package of blue corn tortillas. "You can start cooking these."

I opened drawers until I found a pair of tongs, then started frying the tortillas, a few seconds each side, and stacking them on a plate. I heard Nat open the sideboard.

"Well," she said, "since you're stuck here, you'd better have dinner with us. Help me with this, will you?"

I glanced over my shoulder and saw her and Tony settling a tablecloth on the kitchen table. I turned back to my work, glad he was staying, annoyed that an awkward moment had intruded. Maybe it was me; maybe I was too sensitive. I sighed, giving up on trying to figure it out.

The kitchen was getting warm. Nat had turned on the oven, and now we both started assembling plates of enchiladas, layering the chile sauce, grated cheddar, and onions. A final sprinkling of cheese on top, and they went into the oven. Nat gave the *calabacitas* a stir and added a scattering of corn, then started chopping lettuce and tomatoes for garnish.

"May I help?" I asked.

"No, just relax. You've had a stressful day."

Deprived of busy work, I joined Tony at the table. "Thanks for dealing with this. Good thing you came over."

He nodded. "Guess we're not doing a movie, though. Probably be too late by the time we're done with Walters."

"You haven't mentioned your ca—hic—case," I said. "Did you finish it?"

"All but the clean-up and a boatload of paperwork."

"You found the killer?"

"Killers. Yeah, we spent yesterday rounding them up. That's why I couldn't make it to tea." He gave me an anxious look. "I hope my grandmother didn't try to steamroller you."

"Not exactly. She asked a couple of...uncomfortable questions. She liked the food, though."

Tony grinned. "Especially the cakes, I bet."

"I think the strawberry puffs were her favorite."

"She does like sweet stuff. Thanks for entertaining them."

"Well, we missed you, of course, but I was glad to meet them. Especially Ange—hic—la—she's lovely."

He nodded. "She's a good kid."

"Not so much a kid. She seemed very serious when she talked about a career in nursing."

Tony frowned slightly. "I wish she'd go on and get a bachelor's. She wants an associate's degree because she can get a job faster."

I bit my lip, choosing my words carefully. "College is expensive."

"I told her I'd help. She doesn't want to borrow, though, even from me."

"Well, that's cautious, but it may also be wise."

Manny came in from the garage, wiping dust from his hands. "You still here?" he said, pretending to frown at Tony.

"I got invited to stay for dinner."

"There goes the poker game." Manny came to the table and gave Tony a good-natured buffet on the shoulder. "Coming to the wedding?"

"I haven't had a chance to ask him yet," I said hastily. "We've both been busy."

Tony looked at me "Wedding?"

"Nat and Manny's wedding. It's next—hic—month."

Nat opened the oven and a wave of heat came out, laced with the smell of red chile. I stood up to help her carry food to the table.

"We'll talk," I told Tony, and hurried to collect a basket of warm tortillas. My cheeks were warm, too.

"We need *cervesa*," Manny said, heading to the fridge. He took out a bottle of beer and waved it at me. "You want one, chica?"

"Yes, please."

"How about you, Tony? Or there's sangria, too."

"Beer's great. Thanks."

Nat poured a glass of sangria for herself and joined us at the table. Tony raised his bottle. "Here's to the bride and groom."

I clinked my bottle against his, and saw Manny and Nat's eyes meet across the table as they drank their own private toast. Tony took a bite of enchiladas, then closed his eyes as he chewed, his expression blissful.

"Oh, man," he said. "This is fantastic. I've been eating junk food all week."

"Glad you like it," said Nat, looking pleased.

"Do you cook when you have time?" Manny asked Tony.

"I can grill a burger or boil pasta, but that's about it, other than frozen dinners."

I shook my head slightly, biting back a comment about how unhealthy processed food was. Not everyone liked to cook. I was certainly guilty of taking short cuts myself, now and then.

Time to change the subject. I didn't want to ask Tony about work, because, stress. Likewise the visit from Tommy Swazo. Didn't want to talk about the wedding, either, because the topic was loaded.

"Gina is designing some ads for the tearoom for December," I said, grasping at conversational straws. "I can't believe how—hic —early that stuff has to be done."

"Time flies," Nat said. "It's almost October."

No one had a comment about my advertising plans. Oh, well.

Nat turned to Tony. "I met your sister yesterday. She's charming."

"Oh, thanks. Yeah, she's a peach."

A heavy rapping at the door made me jump. Tony got up, setting his napkin beside his plate.

"That's Walters. 'Scuse me."

I followed him to the door, knowing Walters would want to talk to me, wanting to get it over with. Tony looked out the window, then opened the door.

Walters stood there, cowboy hat crammed low on his forehead, hands stuffed in the pockets of his sheepskin coat. "Sorry to interrupt your dinner," he said, giving Tony a wry look.

"Come in, Detective," said Nat, joining us at the door. "Would you like something to eat?"

"No, thanks. Wife's got dinner waiting at home. I just need to get the facts—the new facts—from Miss Rosings here."

"Why don't you come into the living room?" I said.

"I'll get the knife," Tony said, stepping past Walters to go outside.

I led the detective through to the living room and invited him to sit. He took his tablet out and sank into Manny's favorite chair. Manny hovered at the pass-through to the kitchen, watching. I found that comforting.

I was halfway through describing Tommy Swazo's visit when Tony joined us. He sat beside me on the couch and put the plastic bag holding the knife on the coffee table in front of Walters, who paused to peer at it.

"Looks like the same work as the other one."

"I'm fairly certain it is," I said. "Daniel Swazo made in—hic —inlaid knives."

"And you found this where?"

"Tommy Swazo stuck it in the door as he was leaving," I said. "The door you came through."

Walters looked at Tony, who nodded. "That's where I found it. I bagged it."

Walters frowned, then looked at me. "Better stay away from Mr. Swazo."

"I have every intention of it."

Tony's gaze met mine. Was he going to mention the lab report? Maybe I should make an excuse to leave them together...

Walters turned to me, tilting his head. "But you went back to the flea market this morning."

"Yes. I wanted to see if it would help me remember any details. And I noticed something...it may mean nothing..."

I looked at Tony for guidance. He gave a small nod.

"At the market, Tommy Swazo sells horno bread that his mother bakes. She was there this morning, but not last week. And I noticed—hic—I noticed one shape of bread last week that wasn't there this week. It had a knotwork decoration on top. Tommy had them under the table last week, and I saw him sell one to a young man, but when I asked the price he said it was the last one. Only I don't think it was."

Walters frowned.

"And this morning, another young man with tattoos up his neck came up to Tommy's table, and I heard Tommy say, 'Not today'."

Walters stared at me, silent. My heart thumped.

"So I think there must have been something different ab—hic —about that bread," I concluded. "The one with the knotwork."

It sounded lame to me. Walters's frown deepened. He was still looking at me, but I had the feeling he was seeing something else.

I glanced at Tony. He smiled for just an instant, then his face went back to cop neutral.

Walters looked down at his tablet and poked at the screen a few times, then grunted. "Gotta go. Thanks for the information, Miss Rosings. I'll be in touch."

I stood as he did, surprised. That was it? No questions, no warnings?

Tony followed him out, and remained outside for a few minutes. I returned to the kitchen table and my half-eaten enchiladas. I'd lost my appetite.

"Ellen, I meant it about your staying here tonight," said Manny. "I don't think you should go home."

"The guest room's ready," offered Nat.

"Thanks, but I'd rather sleep in my own bed." Or not sleep, as the case may be. "I don't think Swazo's going to bother me there," I added.

"You didn't think he'd follow you here," said Manny.

I took a swig of my beer, then picked up my fork and pushed some *calabacitas* around my plate. Manny was probably right; there was safety in numbers, at least, though Swazo had come up here pretty boldly. Remembering him standing outside the window, I didn't feel all that safe.

Plus, I was stubborn. As badly as I'd been sleeping at home, I'd probably sleep still worse away from my own bed. And I was damned if I'd be frightened out of my home by a bully, which I was coming to believe Tommy Swazo to be.

Tony came back in, sat down, and started eating again. *His* appetite had not been adversely affected by his colleague's visit.

"Tony, tell Ellen she'd be safer spending the night here," Manny said.

Tony looked at him thoughtfully while he chewed a mouthful and swallowed. "I'm not sure that's true."

"Thank you," I said, giving Manny a repressive look.

"Walters is going to ask for a warrant for Swazo's arrest," Tony added.

I looked at him. "So he made the connection between the bread and the knife."

Tony nodded. "I didn't even have to nudge. Walters is pretty sharp."

"Do you think he'll get a wa—hic—warrant based on my suspicions?"

"There's more than suspicion when Swazo stuck a knife in your door. Plus there's the stuff on Daniel's knife, and his death. It's worth a shot. Depends on what the judge thinks."

I sipped the last of my beer while I watched Tony eat. Nat and Manny had already cleared their plates, and were loading the dishwasher.

Tony wiped the last of the sauce from his plate with a flour tortilla. "You not hungry?"

"Not any more. You want it?"

I nudged my plate toward him and he put it on top of his, then proceeded to clean it. I couldn't help smiling.

"When's the last time you ate a salad?"

"No idea. Want to make me one?"

A frisson shimmied down my spine. Was he asking to come over to my place? I could certainly respond with an invitation...

"Here," Nat said, bringing over the cutting board and scraping the last of the garnish onto the plate. "That'll tide you over."

Tony tilted his head to look up at her sideways. I had to laugh.

"I'd be happy to make you a salad," I said, "but I bet you cou —hic—couldn't do justice to it right now. How about tomorrow night?"

There. I'd done it.

"Sure."

Wow. I'd have to clean up my suite. Or should I feed him in the dining parlor? No, too many uncomfortable memories for us associated with that room.

Tony finished the last bite of my enchiladas, dropped his fork, and held up his hands like a calf-roper who'd done his work. Nat collected the plates, grinning.

"That was awesome," Tony said. "Thank you."

"You're welcome," said Nat. She turned to me. "And *you* are welcome to spend the night. You know that."

"I know. Thanks, but I think I'll rest better at home."

The clock on the microwave showed a few minutes to seven.

Outside the window, night was drifting into puddles under the piñon trees.

"And I should probably go there," I added, getting up. "I'm pretty wiped."

"I'll follow you," Tony said. "And I did request a patrol for you, too."

"Thanks." I smiled at him, then turned to Nat. "Thank you for a great dinner."

Hugs exchanged with Nat and Manny, I gathered my belongings and headed for the door. I paused to peer out the window. It was pretty dark outside. Manny came to turn on the outdoor light.

"You be careful," he said.

"I w—hic—will."

I was glad to have Tony following me home. Maybe I'd invite him in for a nightcap? Except he probably wouldn't want to drink any more before driving. Or maybe I was thinking too hard.

I pulled into my driveway a little ahead of him and parked. As I opened the door I heard the motorcycle's engine shut off, a gesture of courtesy to my neighbors. Tony had done that before, coasting up the driveway, though it really wasn't necessary. I smiled.

The house was dark; I'd forgotten to leave a light on. I got out of the car, shouldered my purse, and stepped onto the *portal*.

A shadow moved between me and the door. I froze. The shadow lunged toward me, faster than I'd have thought possible, and in the dim light something glinted like a knife.

12

A "POP, POP" STARTLED ME as I jumped backward. The shadow stumbled, dropped to one knee, said something I didn't understand in a low, masculine voice, then slumped forward.

"Ellen!" Tony shouted behind me. "Get back!"

I backed up and nearly bumped into Tony as he got off his bike. He ignored me, brushing past me, moving forward, his attention on the man on the ground.

What just happened?

Tony's hands were out in front of him and though I couldn't see it, from his stance I realized he was holding a gun. My heart, which was already racing, pounded even faster.

The man on the ground groaned. I began to fear I knew who it was.

"Turn on the porch light," Tony called.

I hurried to the *portal* that ran alongside the kitchen, staying well away from my would-be attacker. At the back door I opened my purse to get out my keys.

That's when I noticed my hands were shaking. My breath rasped as I fumbled to find the keys, to get the right one into the lock. I heard Tony talking in a low voice, saying police codes.

I finally got the door open and reached in to turn on the lights. I hit the whole bank of switches, lighting up both the outdoors and the hallway.

Sprawled beside my car lay Tommy Swazo, on his side, not moving.

"Crap," said Tony.

An open knife lay by Swazo's hand, the hilt done in red and black. I caught my breath, took a step toward him.

What just happened?

"Stay back!" Tony stared at the man on the ground with intense concentration, one hand still holding the gun on him, the other holding a cell phone. "Is that Swazo?"

"Yes," I said. I was shaking. "H-he doesn't look like he's breathing. Should I do something?"

"Go inside. Help's on the way."

I couldn't leave Tony alone with that man. I feared—irrationally, no doubt—that Swazo would rise up, like the villain in some movie who should have been dead but wasn't, after all.

Not that I'd be able to do anything about it if he did.

But he would not be getting up. Swazo's eyes stared, unmoving. Blood spread in a gradually widening pool beneath him, glinting on the edges of the gravel. And I began to understand what had happened.

Tony had saved me from being stabbed. Swazo had meant to kill me.

A siren sounded in the distance. We held still, waiting, listening to it increase in volume until the sound became painful, then abruptly shut off. Headlights swung into my driveway and crunched to a stop. Red and blue lights flashed, hurting my eyes, making me dizzy.

"Police," said a voice over a loudspeaker.

"Aragón," Tony shouted back. "I called it in."

"OK, stay there."

A car door opened and closed. More sirens were approaching. A uniformed officer walked up to Tony.

"Get up," the officer said to Swazo, who didn't respond.

The officer looked up at me. He was young—probably younger than me.

"She's the homeowner," Tony said.

The officer moved around behind Swazo and nudged his leg with a foot. No response. Kneeling, one hand on his holstered gun, the officer reached his other hand to Swazo's neck, then murmured something I didn't catch.

"Crap," Tony said again. He lowered his gun.

More police arrived, then paramedics. Tony stood talking to

a growing circle of cops while the paramedics worked on Swazo. He looked stressed.

Realizing I wasn't going to get near Tony any time soon, I went inside to the kitchen and found Julio's stash of coffee, which I raided to make a pot for the responders. I got the beans ground and the coffee maker started, though I was still shaky. I leaned on the counter while I waited for the coffee to brew, taking deep breaths.

Swazo was dead. Tony had killed him. Oh, God.

By the time I went back out through the kitchen door with a tray of mugs, I was a little steadier. The crowd had grown. Yellow tape was strung between the posts of the *portal* and the lilacs, surrounding my car and Swazo and enclosing the back door of the house. The paramedics were packing up, unhurried, and in their place crime scene technicians were working.

Several of the newcomers were dressed in plain clothes, and one of them was talking to Tony. I went around the south side, skirting the police tape, and made my way toward them as I handed out coffee.

The plainclothes guy looked up at me. "Thanks," he said, taking a mug.

Tony glanced at the tray and shook his head. He looked haggard.

"Can I talk to you?" I asked him.

"Not now," said the plainclothes guy. "You're the property owner?"

"Yes."

"We need to get your statement. Wilson, come here," he called, and another officer joined us.

Wilson took the last mug of coffee and asked me politely if there was a place where we could talk. I left the tray on the bench —the only piece of furniture that was outside the yellow tape— and led him into the kitchen. It was chilly now and I was shivering off and on, though it might just be reaction. We sat at the break table and he took notes while I told him what had happened.

He made no comment while I talked. When I had finished, he looked up.

"Did you know who the man was when you first saw him?"

"No, it was dark. All I saw was his shape and the glint of the knife."

"You're sure it was the knife?"

"I don't know what else it could be."

"All right. Thanks. I'll need your phone number in case we have more questions."

I gave it to him. He left, and I started another pot of coffee, and one of tea for me.

The tea was ready first. I chose a pretty china cup and saucer —white and cobalt blue, with gold embellishments—and drank a cup by myself at the table while I waited for the coffee to brew. My stomach remained in a tight knot, but the tea soothed my agitated spirits.

I wanted to talk with Tony. I didn't care if I never saw any of the others again, but I'd give them all of Julio's coffee if it would give me a chance—just a minute—to talk with Tony.

When the coffee maker stopped dripping, I took the pot outside. The crowd had thinned a bit, and I was worried Tony might be gone, but I spotted him in a circle of cops, both uniformed and plainclothes. I went up to them, offering with a gesture to fill mugs. Several were held out to me.

Over by my car, a familiar form in a sheepskin jacket was talking to the crime scene techs. Walters must be angry; I would have been, in his place. I avoided making eye contact with him.

An older man in a beige wool overcoat was talking to Tony, who nodded occasionally, looking rather drawn. I filled mugs for those who had them, then stood waiting until the man in beige finally acknowledged me.

"May I speak to Detective Aragón for a minute?" I said.

"He's coming to the station," said the man, frowning.

"This won't take long."

The man's eyes narrowed, but he gave a curt nod and turned to Officer Wilson. I stepped over to Tony.

"I just wanted to thank you," I said in a low voice. "Are you in trouble?"

He gave a tiny, helpless shrug. "I killed a guy." His face was stoic, but his voice was miserable. His gaze drifted to where Swazo lay.

I put a hand on his shoulder. "You saved my life."

He looked at me. "Well, that makes it worth it," he whispered hoarsely.

His dark eyes were filled with pain. There were too many others around, or I would have hugged him. Instead I squeezed his shoulder.

"Call me. It doesn't matter how late."

He swallowed, then nodded. The man in beige came back and took Tony away to a sedan.

My God, were they going to arrest him? No, that couldn't be it. But why the car, when he had his bike?

Some cop thing, I decided. There were traditions, and procedures, that I knew nothing about. I watched the car drive away, feeling like crying.

I was damned if I'd cry in front of all these strangers, though. I poured the last of the coffee into the nearest mugs and went back to the kitchen to start another pot.

There, in private, I allowed myself a moment to go quietly to pieces. Then I blew my nose, wiped my eyes, and went out to pick up the empty mugs that had been collecting on the tray I'd left out there. I loaded mugs into the dishwasher, filled the tray with fresh ones, and when the coffee was ready I took another round outside. It looked like things were winding down, though who knew how long the techs would be working.

Walters, standing to one side with a couple of the uniforms, accepted a mug of coffee and gave me a wry look. If he was hoping for an apology from me, he wasn't going to get it. Frankly, I was relieved, if not exactly glad, that Swazo was dead, though it would have been nice if he hadn't died on my property.

Walters sidled over to me. "So, you want to tell me what happened?"

"I gave my statement to Officer Wilson."

Walters's eyebrows went up. "Ouch. Why're you mad at me?"

I sighed. "I'm just tired. This has been a long, awful day."

"You got that right. By the way, looks like you were right about Danny Swazo being dumped on the frontage road. I talked to the flea market staff and one of them saw him and Tommy fighting in the parking lot that afternoon."

"Oh." I couldn't think of anything else to say. I looked over at Tommy Swazo, who had killed his brother with his hands. Being right gave me no sense of triumph.

"Thanks for the coffee." Walters raised his mug and then turned away, earning my sincere gratitude for possibly the first time.

I gave out the rest of the coffee, making sure the techs had some. I recognized one of them—a tall young man with blond hair and glasses who had been here the night Sylvia died. He smiled, thanked me, and went back to work.

There was nothing more for me to do. My car was once again hostage to a crime scene, so I couldn't leave. I was too tired to go anywhere anyway. I went around to everyone that was left, inviting them to use the bathrooms before I locked up for the night. I went back to the kitchen and cleaned up while several of them took advantage of this offer. As I was cleaning the coffee maker, the first of the news crews showed up.

Publicity be damned. Sorry, Gina. I'm not in the mood.

I said goodnight to the tech with glasses as he went back out, and locked the door behind him. If the police wanted me, they had my number. I went upstairs to my suite.

My cell phone rang; one of the news crews. I let it go to voicemail.

I had a text message from my neighbor on the corner, Katie Hutchins.

Saw police lights. Everything OK?

No, everything was not OK. I sighed, composed a brief,

reassuring answer and sent it.

I wanted to text Tony, but that was useless. Whatever he was doing at the police station, he probably didn't need me interrupting him.

Nat. I'd better let her know. I was tempted to text, but she'd only call me back so I might as well get it over with. The phone rang again, a number I didn't know. I waited for it to go to voicemail, then called Nat's number and curled up in my chair. When she answered, I gave her a brief account.

She was horrified, naturally. Swazo was a maniac. Manny was right, I should have spent the night.

"No," I said. "If I hadn't come home tonight, Swazo might have caught me alone another time. Tony saved my life. I was lucky he was here."

"Is Tony there now?"

"No, they took him to the police station."

"Do you need some company? I could come over."

I gave an exasperated chuckle. "I've got plenty of company, thanks. I'm ready for some quiet."

"Call me if you change your mind. Manny will come get you. Don't drive to us."

I can't. My car is in a crime scene.

On that thought, I remembered the gifts I'd bought for Nat and Manny at the flea market. They were still in the trunk of my car. I'd have to rescue them, but later. They'd be all right there for now.

"Thanks," I told her. "I'll call."

We said good night, and I set the phone to pager mode and put it on the table beside me where I could see the caller ID. It rang a few more times; either numbers I had marked as the press or numbers I didn't know. I ignored them all.

Disinclined to move, I pulled my lap rug over myself and curled up to wait for Tony to call. It wasn't late, but stress had taken its toll on me. I felt myself sliding into a doze. I had one last coherent thought as my tired eyes drifted closed.

The hiccups were gone.

13

I KNOW I DREAMED, and that the dreams weren't fun, but they weren't scary enough to wake me and the sound of the cell phone buzzing its way across the table chased them away. I sat up, blinking, grabbed the phone, and glanced at the caller ID.

"Tony! Are you all right?"

There was a long pause. "Yeah, I'm OK."

"What happened? Why—"

"I had to be interviewed. Standard procedure."

It was his tough guy voice. I usually didn't have much luck communicating with him when I heard it.

"Tony, I'm so sorry."

"Not your fault."

"Listen, do you want to come over? We could talk..."

Another long pause. "I'd better not. Not tonight."

I swallowed. "OK. You still want to come for dinner tomorrow?"

"I don't know. Sorry, I'm just..."

"It's OK, Tony," I said after a moment. "It's OK. If it helps, I think you did the right thing. There's no question."

"Thanks."

"They've got to follow procedure, right? That's all this is."

"Yeah."

I tried to think of something more to say, something to encourage him. It seemed obvious to me that Tony had done the only thing he could do.

"See, they have to decide if it was legal," he said, his voice tight. "Doesn't matter if it was right. If I acted outside the law..."

"You were defending me! He would have killed me—"

"Maybe. That's what you and I think."

My stomach sank. "What can I do?"

"Nothing. You've done what you can."

I closed my eyes. He sounded depressed, which I could understand. I couldn't begin to imagine how terrible I would feel if I had killed someone, even if it had been the right course of action.

On top of that, a Sword of Damocles was hanging over Tony. He might lose his job. Maybe even go to jail.

"Call me tomorrow, OK?" I said. "If you have time."

"Oh, I'll have time," he said with a bitter laugh. "I'm on leave for three days."

"Oh, Tony..."

"It's OK. It's just that I can't wrap up my case. Not allowed to work on anything."

I squeezed my eyes shut, fighting tears. I couldn't melt down, not now. That would just make everything worse. Tony needed support.

I swallowed. "Maybe you can get some rest. You've been working so hard."

"Yeah. Well. Speaking of rest, I'd better let you go."

I wanted to protest, to keep him talking. My tired brain couldn't come up with a way to do that.

"Sleep well, then," I told him. "Talk to you tomorrow."

"Yeah."

A click told me he'd hung up. I put the phone down and cried.

Daniel Swazo did not visit me that night. Hiccup-free, I went to bed without a sleeping pill. I was immensely relieved that the spasms were gone, but too sad to celebrate. My dreams were restless although not horrible, and I couldn't remember them when I woke.

It was early, but I got up. Some little sound from downstairs must have alerted me to Julio's arrival. I checked my phone, discarded several texts from reporters, answered two from Gina and Kris. Nothing from Tony.

Wanting company, I dressed in jeans and a sweater, slid my phone into a pocket, and went down. I started a pot of tea brewing in the pantry, then went into the kitchen, where I found Julio looking at the clean mugs in the dishwasher.

"Have a party last night?" he asked, turning to me.

"It wasn't on the news?"

"I didn't watch the news. Why do I have a bad feeling?"

I sighed, grabbed one of the clean mugs, and helped myself to his freshly-brewed coffee. "I owe you a pound of this. I made a bunch of it last night, for half the cops in SFPD."

"You found another body?"

"Not exactly."

We sat down with coffee and I told him about Swazo and Tony and all the rest. His frown deepened as he listened.

"How can I help?"

"I don't think you can, but thanks." I finished my coffee and stood. "Oh, the media might show up. Just ignore them."

"Right."

"What do I owe you for the coffee?"

"Nada. My gift."

"You don't have to do that."

"I want to." He looked at me with serious eyes. "You've had a rough time lately. It's the least I can do."

I smiled and gave him a quick hug. "Thanks, Julio. You're a prince."

He grinned. "Hey, your hiccups are gone!"

"Yeah. I found the ultimate cure."

I collected my tea and went upstairs to my office, where I sat down with a cuppa and my messages from Saturday. My phone buzzed, goosing me. I took it out, saw a number I didn't know, and set it on the desk.

Resisting the urge to call Tony, I went through the messages. None were urgent. I returned a couple of calls, then checked my email, where I found a bunch of inquiries from the press and a message from Sonja at the Archives:

Ellen -

Here are the files that came up first on a search for Colt
and Hidalgo. These are probably your best bet, but if you
want more I saved the search results. I have not gone
through these files to identify the references.

Three files were attached: a diary belonging to one Manuel
Hidalgo, a collection of letters addressed to Seraphina Ruiz, and
a sales register from Seligman's Mercantile. It would take time to
go through them and find the references, if indeed there were
any. Sometimes these files didn't include the search keys they
turned up under.

On any other day I would have been excited to receive this
lead, but I didn't have the energy to devote to needle-hunting.
My thoughts were on Tony, wishing he'd call, trying to figure out
ways to help him. I saved the files, set the email aside, and
turned back to my "to-do" pile.

On top was a message from Willow, from last week. I'd
already talked to her. I dropped it in the recycling bin, but then
remembered that I wanted to do a cleansing on the house. Now,
more than ever, I wanted to make sure no hostile spirits were
hanging around. Willow might have suggestions.

Not wanting to talk on the phone, I sent her a brief email. I
assumed she'd heard the news, and told her it was related to the
Swazo case. That should be enough information, I figured.

Next on the stack was the flyer from the Hospice Center. A
wince of guilt went through me—I'd said I would make a
donation. Well, no time like the present. I got out my checkbook
and wrote out a check for fifty dollars. Not as much as I'd have
liked to donate, but as much as I could afford. I could always
send more later, if business continued to be good.

I pulled the check out of the book and slipped it into an
envelope. As I was writing "The Hospice Center" on the outside,
I remembered I'd made an appointment with Loren for Monday.

Was it Monday? Yes. My sense of order and normalcy had
been disrupted to the point I wasn't sure of the day. That was

bad.

So, appointment with Loren. I looked on my calendar and verified the time: eleven o'clock. I could take the check with me and save a stamp.

If I went. Maybe another day would be better.

Except a talk with Loren would probably be a big relief right now. I could tell him about Swazo. He already knew about my dreams about Daniel.

A memory arose of Loren and his sister, dressed for tea, smiling. Loren's smile especially warm.

I'd go. If nothing else, I needed to set some boundaries.

The moment that thought went through my mind, my feelings crystallized.

I liked Loren. A lot. He was very attractive, and he got my jokes. I could even see myself dating him, if circumstances were different.

But Tony and I had unfinished business. Despite our differences, we were involved, at least emotionally, and now there was this—mess—to resolve.

I checked the cell phone again, but there was nothing new. I'd have heard it buzz.

Footsteps on the stairs roused me from musing. I tucked the envelope under my phone and got up to refill my teacup, meeting Kris in the doorway.

She had on black jeans and turtleneck, with a silver ankh on a black leather cord around her neck and tiny ankh earrings.

"Good morning," I said. "You don't usually come in on Mondays."

"I saw the ten o'clock news last night. What the hell happened?"

"Tea?" I offered, filling my own cup.

"Yes. And by the way, there's a television crew camped out front."

I grimaced. We took our tea out to the sitting area by the front window and I told her the story. In exchange, she told me what the television stations had reported.

"Officer-involved shooting. One man dead. Identity withheld pending notification of next of kin. They had a good shot of the back yard, with yellow tape and all."

"Great," I said, and took another swallow of tea.

Next of kin. Poor Mrs. Swazo. Another son gone. Did she have any other kids, or was she all alone now?

"I noticed you didn't talk to the media," Kris said.

"No, and I don't plan to."

"Gina will yell."

I pressed my fingertips against my eyes. "I can't deal with them right now."

"OK. I'd better go pull the messages, then. Do you want me to answer any of them?"

"Not from the press."

"Want to give me a statement for them, in case one gets through?"

I thought for a minute. "Tell them...no, that would be a lie. Just refer them to the police."

"Right."

Kris stood, then picked up her cup and saucer. "Is there any tea left?"

"I think we drank it all." I lifted the lid of the teapot. "Yep. I'll go make some more."

I followed Kris into her office and left my cup on the credenza. "I have an appointment at eleven, so I'll be going out," I said. "I could take Saturday's deposit if it's ready."

Kris nodded, already on the phone. I took the pot downstairs, made more tea, snooped on Julio (making scones), and went back up to check my cell. More unknowns, nothing from Tony.

The phone rang as I was putting it down. Nat, calling to check up on me. We talked, and she asked if I wanted her to come in.

"No, thanks. Julio and Kris are here. Um, I don't think I'll come to work on the dress tonight."

"That's all right, but please call me if you want company. Or call Gina. Don't isolate yourself, Ellen."

"No, I won't. I'm going to talk to that counselor today."

"Good! Tell him I said hello."

We said goodbye, then I looked for something to occupy me until it was time to leave. Gina had emailed me proofs for an ad campaign for the spirit tour/tea combo. It was tasteful and intriguing, but I wondered if I should ditch it in view of last night's events. Tommy Swazo's death could be bad news for the tearoom. There hadn't been a shooting here before.

What was I thinking? Yes, there had—Captain Dusenberry's!

14

TOMMY SWAZO HAD DIED less than ten yards from where Captain Dusenberry had died, both of gunshot wounds. A shiver went through me as I recalled the sound of Tony's gun. Two shots. The Captain had also been shot twice.

Could this house be a vortex of violence? Would I never be free of the shadow of death?

I shook myself. It wasn't that bad. It seemed so right now, but we'd recover. The story would fade, and the tearoom I'd worked so hard to establish would go on. It had to.

I didn't want to think about what would happen if the tearoom failed. I'd be in debt forever. I'd have to sell the house and get a job, probably as a teacher. I dreaded having to deal with the current school system. The mere thought nudged me closer to depression.

Kris came in with the bank bag. "Saturday was a good day," she said.

"Good. Have we had cancellations?"

"A few."

I nodded. "Not surprising. I just hope it doesn't turn into an avalanche."

"Mrs. Olavssen booked a reservation for tomorrow."

I winced. Leave it to the Bird Woman to be the first on the scene. She'd wheedle me for information about the shooting. Maybe I'd spend Tuesday upstairs. In bed.

"Well, it's nice to have loyal patrons," I said, trying to look at the bright side.

Kris smiled. "Have a good lunch."

Lunch? Oh, yeah. Food. I'd kind of skipped breakfast.

I didn't feel hungry. Maybe I'd stop for a bite after seeing

Loren. Fetching a tweed jacket from my suite, I slipped my phone into one pocket and the envelope for the Hospice Center in the other, and headed out with the bank bag.

At the foot of the stairs, I heard voices from the kitchen. Curious, I peeked in and saw a vaguely familiar blonde guy leaning against the counter, watching Julio work. A bosun-necked shirt exposed a tempting glimpse of male shoulder. He looked up and smiled, and I remembered: he was Julio's roommate.

"Andre," I said, going over to shake hands. "Nice to see you."

"Hi, Ellen. Julio wanted some company, and I had the day off. Hope you don't mind."

"As long as you don't share our trade secrets with Santacafé. How's it going over there?"

"Pretty well."

Julio glanced up. "He's in line for a promotion."

"Is he? Congratulations!"

"Thanks," Andre said.

"I'm going out," I told Julio. "Need me to pick up anything?"

"Still making this week's list. There's nothing urgent."

"I'll walk out with you," Andre said.

I was about to say that it wasn't necessary, but he was already at the kitchen's back door, so I smiled my thanks and went out. I hesitated at the sight of two men loitering in my driveway. One of them looked familiar—a reporter?

Andre stepped between me and them as they started toward me. "Ms. Rosings isn't commenting," he said, arms out in a herding-away gesture.

Amazed and grateful, I made a beeline for my car. A dark patch on the ground made me freeze. Carefully, I stepped around it, got in the driver's seat, and threw Andre a grateful look. He smiled as I started the engine and backed out past the scowling newsmen.

How kind of Andre, and of Julio! I didn't doubt for a second that my chef had called his friend in to help buffer me from the press.

The day was pretty, though rather chilly, with large puffy clouds in the sky. I rolled down my window as I drove through town, imagining I detected the scent of rain. I'd left a bit early, so I stopped by the bank first, then headed for the Hospice Center.

Loren was in the lobby when I came in, dressed in a nice shirt and slacks, sage green over beige. He smiled, but gave me a rather searching look.

"Good to see you, Ellen. I half expected you to cancel."

"I gather you saw the news."

He nodded. "Let's go on back."

The little lounge was again empty. I couldn't help a sigh of relief as I sank into the sofa with a cup of coffee. This place felt safe.

"I'm glad you decided to come," Loren said.

"Well, I couldn't cancel. I promised to tell you about the Bird Woman."

"Bird Woman?"

"Our regular customer. The one who played the Andrews Sisters."

"Oh, yes. Why is she the Bird Woman?"

"Well, she looks like one. Oh, my aunt said to tell you hello," I said. "Do you remember her? Natasha Wheeler?"

"Of course. She was there on Saturday, right?"

"Yes, she was."

He smiled. "Please tell her hello back for me."

"I will."

I swallowed some coffee, then took the envelope from my pocket. "Here's a donation for the Center."

"Thank you," he said, setting it on the table between us. "How are you doing?"

I sighed and stared at the mug in my hands. "I've been better."

"There wasn't much detail on the news."

"It was Daniel Swazo's brother."

"Oh!"

I told him all of it, trusting his discretion. He listened,

nodding now and then but not interrupting. My recitation was pretty incoherent, because I kept backtracking to explain things like why Tony was having supper at Nat's house.

"We've been trying to get together for a movie, and he finally had a night off, so he came over but in the meantime Swazo was there," I said, not very coherently. "You met Detective Aragón, didn't you?"

"No."

"Oh." I drank some coffee, suddenly embarrassed.

"You've known him for a while, I gather?"

"Since the tearoom opened last spring. He investigated the murder. The first murder," I added bitterly.

"I see."

"Do you think I'm a corpse magnet?"

Loren looked startled. "A what?"

"It's just that there've been so many murders, in less than a year."

"Not all at the tearoom."

"True, but—"

"And this last one wasn't a murder."

"I hope not. It depends what the legal experts think."

He was silent. I drank some more coffee, feeling depressed. It had been good to talk it out, but that didn't change the fact that Tony was in trouble, possibly big trouble, because of me.

I looked up and found Loren watching me, a slight, worried frown on his face. I'd confounded him.

Way to go, Rosings.

I put my mug down. "Thank you for listening. You've been a big help, but perhaps I shouldn't come again."

Dismay fleeted across his face, quickly replaced by studied calm. "Why not?"

"Well, I think maybe there are some personal feelings going on."

He blinked, then relaxed into a wry smile. "I've always had a terrible poker face."

"It's OK."

He stood up. "No, I apologize. I can't counsel you any more, in this situation. I should have...." He paced a couple of steps toward the kitchenette and back. "If you want a different counselor, there are others here. Or if you'd rather go somewhere else, I can make some recommendations, but I'm afraid they're not free."

"Thanks. I'll think about that."

Conscious of a sense of disappointment, I stood and carried my mug to the kitchenette. Loren leaned back against a counter, watching me from a distance.

"I do like you, Ellen. I'd like to know you better." I turned to face him, and he held up a hand. "I understand—don't worry. I'd still like to be friends, if that's an option."

"You'd settle for that?"

"Sure." His gaze on me was soft, making me doubt whether he really could settle, even if he thought he could. "Beats nothing," he added.

"I don't want to string you along."

"I'm a grown-up. And I do have my eyes open."

Pretty eyes, too. Amazing clear blue. I hoped I wouldn't hurt him.

"Well," I said slowly, "I'm kind of in one-day-at-a-time mode."

"That works."

We gazed at each other for a long while. It was perfectly comfortable, which rather surprised me. I could stare into his eyes without worrying about...anything, really.

"I'd better go," I said, without moving.

"OK."

"Thanks for understanding."

"Thanks for not being mad. I hope you're not mad?"

"No."

"I notice your hiccups are gone."

"Yes. But I don't recommend this particular cure."

He chuckled. "As long as you can joke, it's not too bad."

I went back to the couch and collected my purse. Loren

followed, still keeping a careful distance. Considerate of him.

"Maybe in a week or so I'll call and we can go to lunch. Dutch treat," he added as I shot him a look, then he grinned. "I still want to hear about the Bird Woman."

I laughed. He walked with me out to the lobby. A whisper of evergreen scent followed us.

"Good to see you, Ellen," he said at the door. "Let me know if you want some referrals."

"Thank you. I will."

I got in my car, feeling a bit light-headed, probably from coffee and tea and emotion and no food. Not being in the mood to ponder about where to eat, I headed for a favorite standby: the French Pastry Shop at La Fonda. It was autumn and they were serving French onion soup.

While I was enjoying my soup and a small salad, my phone buzzed. I took it out to check the caller: Tony.

"Hi," I said, my heart beating fast all at once.

"Hi."

"How's it going?"

"OK. Nothing new."

I bit my lip. What to ask? What not to ask?

"Things OK with you?" he said.

"Yeah. I've been dodging the press."

"Sorry."

"Not your fault," I said, smiling. He'd said the same thing to me last night. "I've got people running interference for me. It's pretty sweet of them."

"Not surprised. People like you."

"So, are you coming for dinner?"

Long pause. I held my breath.

"Sure, I guess."

Oh man. Was he building a wall? But at least he was willing to see me.

"What do you like?"

"Anything. I'm sure I'll like whatever you make. Should I bring some wine or beer or something?"

"I've got wine. If you want something else, feel free."

"OK. What time?"

"Seven? Or would you rather eat earlier?"

"Seven's fine. See you then."

Click.

"OK, bye," I said, knowing he was gone.

I finished my lunch, pondering what to make for him. Something he couldn't or wouldn't eat out, and something that didn't involve baking, since I didn't have an oven upstairs and I didn't want to dine downstairs.

Steak was too easy, and I didn't know if he liked fish, so I settled on chicken. Maybe with a nice risotto, and something from the wine cellar. I thought through my recipes and decided on a cream sauce with shallots and brandy that I'd made up myself.

On the way out, I made the obligatory inspection of the pastry case. Having plenty of sweets on hand at the tearoom, I passed on the napoleons and tarts, but I bought a baguette and, as an afterthought, a couple of croissants. I loved croissants for breakfast, and they weren't on the tearoom's menu.

As I walked to my car I remembered the doll and the knife I'd bought for Nat and Manny. Better get them out of the trunk now; if the press were staking out my house, I wouldn't want to take the time in my driveway. I retrieved the bag that held them both and set it beside the bread on the passenger seat.

I was having second thoughts about the knife, though. It was beautiful, but I wouldn't have minded never seeing any of Daniel's knives again. Maybe I'd set it aside and find something else for Manny.

Next stop: grocery store. Chicken, shallots, cream, salad fixings, and some fruit and cheese. And yogurt—I was almost out.

It was nearly one when I reached the tearoom. Julio and Andre must have been watching for me, because Andre came out of the kitchen as I parked, shooed off the reporters again, and helped me carry in the groceries. I followed him into the kitchen.

"Thanks," I said as we piled bags on the counter. "I owe you a nice meal."

"No, no. Glad to help."

"Mind if I go, boss?" Julio asked. "I'm caught up."

"Go ahead. See you tomorrow."

They left, locking the kitchen door behind them. I headed upstairs with my collection of bags and met Kris at the top of the stairs.

"You headed out? Here's the bank bag," I said, shuffling grocery bags.

"Yeah, unless you need me to stay. Want a hand with those?"

"I've got it. Thanks. Watch out for the press."

I put away the groceries and the gifts, then checked my desk for messages. Rather than write a bunch of message slips, Kris had printed out a list—apparently from a spreadsheet—of all the media people who had called. Just looking at it depressed me; I stuck it in my "later" pile.

There were a couple of regular messages, and an email from Willow. She hoped I wasn't distressed about Tommy Swazo (how could I not be?), she could recommend a shaman who would cleanse the house but she wanted to talk about it first, and the spirit/tea combo tours were almost completely booked. Could we add some more dates? Perhaps Thursdays?

Wow. Not even October yet.

I pulled up the reservations chart and saw that the dining parlor was free on three out of four Thursdays in October. I filled in the same time slot Willow had booked for Wednesdays and Fridays, and an earlier slot on the one conflicting day, then sent the list to Willow for approval. I'd have to contact Mr. Quentin, too.

While I had the reservation chart up, I glanced at the current week. A bit sparse, but that wasn't surprising. It might have been worse. Thank goodness for the spirit tours.

Was my beloved establishment doomed to become "that haunted tearoom?"

I sighed, dashed off an email to Tony, warning him that the

press was hanging around, then headed across the hall to do a whirlwind clean-up on my suite. Laundry, floors, bathroom, kitchenette. I hadn't been this thorough in months.

The table looked a little stark, so decided I wanted flowers and went downstairs. I was at the back door, shears and a vase in hand, when I remembered the press.

I looked out through the lights that surrounded the door. Yes, there they were—hanging around at the end of the driveway. Frowning, I went down the hall to the front door, and peeked out the window lights there.

A news van was parked at the curb. Past experience had taught me they were there to do a remote broadcast, probably on the six-o'clock news.

Most annoying. I wanted flowers on my table, and fresh thyme and rosemary for the dinner, but I wasn't willing to run the gauntlet to get them. I went into the main parlor and raided the vases in Rose for half a dozen pink and red roses. I'd be doing fresh flowers for the tearoom tomorrow, anyway.

As I carried the vase upstairs, I wondered if I was a coward. Would it hurt me to talk to the press? Gina always said there was no such thing as bad publicity, but I didn't know. This situation was different. With Tony's job at risk, I didn't want to rock the boat.

I set the vase in the center of the table, then took a long, hot, luxurious shower. A pretty flowered skirt and a long-sleeved top made me feel feminine but not formal. Brush hair, touch of makeup, and I was presentable.

It was time to start dinner. I put on some soft music, took a bottle of red wine out of the cellar and opened it, and got out my apron. Rice first. I didn't have the energy for risotto, I decided, so I set some basmati to steaming, put together the salad, and was ready to start the main dish.

It called for brandy. I ran downstairs to steal some of Julio's, and on the way back stepped into my office for a quick check of my email and phone (nothing from Tony). Back in my suite, I took out my recipe card, opened the window to evacuate the smell of raw shallots, and set to work.

My mood was lifting; cooking always did me good. Since the tearoom had opened, my meals at home had been less elaborate than before. It felt good to stretch the culinary muscles.

Leaving the shallots gently sautéeing in butter, I went out into the hallway. The sheers over the west window were golden and I could feel the warmth of the setting sun pouring through them. I stood before the window for a couple of minutes, basking. It felt so good I wanted to curl up in one of the chairs for a nap, but there wasn't time.

I had just added the brandy and turned down the burner to simmer the chicken when I heard a knock downstairs. I pulled off my apron and hurried down, pausing at the foot of the stairs to look at both doors, because I wasn't sure which to go to. The back door had a doorbell, but it wasn't obvious and I didn't remember whether Tony knew where to find it.

As it happened, he was at the front, blocking the last rays of sunshine from the lights on one side of the door. I found out why he was standing so close when I opened the door and a reporter tried to shove a microphone at me.

"No comment," I said. "Come in, Detective."

Tony stepped in and pushed the door closed behind him. I locked it, then led him down the hall. Behind us, the reporter watched through the lights.

"Sorry about that," I said. "I'd have thought they would leave after the six o'clock broadcast. Did they give you grief?"

"I don't let them," Tony said.

"Let's step into the kitchen for a moment."

He shot me a sidelong look. "Don't want them to see us going upstairs?"

"Do you?"

"Yeah, you're right. It would just pour gas on the fire."

They'd probably make hay with Tony's visit anyway. I was glad I didn't have a television.

I went into the side hall, but stopped outside the butler's pantry. Out of view of both doors, and the small window in the pantry was curtained.

"I don't really need anything from the kitchen," I said, turning to him.

"Oh."

"I just wanted to...before we get busy with dinner...I wanted to thank you."

The the ghost of a smile fleeted across his face. He looked so sad.

"Are you OK?" I asked.

Tony shrugged. "It's hard. I can't work, and I want to finish that case."

"You can't even do paperwork?"

He shook his head. "Not for three days."

"Oh." I bit back an apology; we didn't need to keep having that exchange.

He leaned against the wall, hands shoved in his pockets. "Walters called me."

"Is he still working on his case?"

"Yeah. But he's having trouble. Swazo lived on the reservation."

"FBI jurisdiction."

"Right. When it was just Daniel's death, not on the res, he could work it, but now that it's a drug operation...he's supposed to turn the case over to the Feds, but they won't do anything with it. They're tapped. He wants to finish it."

"What a mess."

"Yeah."

Outside, a siren went wailing by. We both looked up, listening until it faded.

"You hungry?" I asked.

"Not really."

"How about a glass of wine, then?"

He raised weary eyes to mine. "That sounds good."

We went upstairs without turning on the lights. Dusk was falling outside, but there was enough light to see our way. A clean soap smell reached me as he walked beside me. I opened the door to my suite, and Tony paused on the threshold, smiling crookedly.

"Last time I was in here you weren't too happy about it."

Oh, yes. The night he'd tossed my suite.

Maybe there weren't any rooms in the house that didn't have bad memories for us.

"Red or white?" I asked.

"Red."

"Have a seat."

He settled himself in my chair as I closed the door. I checked on the chicken, then poured the wine.

"Dinner's almost ready," I said as I handed him a glass.

"Smells great."

I sat in the other chair. "Have you talked to your mom?"

He grimaced. "Not yet. I left her a message."

I watched him take a big swallow of wine. Surely his mother would support him, wouldn't she?

He gazed at the wineglass in his hands. "She'll say it's a sin, and nag me to go confess."

Oh.

"Would that make you feel better?" I asked.

He thought about it, drank more wine. "No."

"It's not like you had a choice," I said softly.

"No, but I wish he hadn't died."

Did I agree? Yes, for Tony's sake, I could wish that. Even though Tommy Swazo's death had solved a problem for me, I couldn't be glad that it had happened. Tony looked so hurt.

I put my hand over his. He was still for a moment, then lifted his fingers to thread them through mine. A tingle spread through my palm and up my wrist.

My kitchen timer went off. Tony slid his hand away. I swallowed frustration and stood.

"Let's eat."

I brought the food to the table and closed the window against the evening chill. Tony helped himself to salad. I watched while he tasted it.

"Good," he said, nodding. "What's in this?"

"Pears, goat cheese, toasted pecans. I usually use poppy seeds, but I didn't know if you might have to pass a drug test."

He swallowed and reached for his wine. "Not unless I get arrested."

I gave myself a mental kick, but couldn't help asking, "That's not very likely, is it?"

"I don't know. Been a lot of bad press about officer-involved shootings."

"Do you want to talk about it, or should I shut up?"

He gave me a surprised look, then a brief smile. "It's OK. But there isn't anything new to say, really."

"Would my testimony help?"

"Let's hope it doesn't come to that."

He finished his wine and cut into his chicken. I brought the bottle to the table and filled his glass.

"Walters put in a good word for me," Tony added.

"That was nice of him."

"He's a good guy."

"I believe you. I'm just seeing him from a different perspective."

Tony looked up at me. "Do cops make you feel threatened?"

"Some do. In some situations."

He sighed. "We're supposed to be the heroes. Serve and protect."

"A lot of folks have forgotten that, I think."

"Yeah. Folks on both sides." He took a bite of chicken, then closed his eyes and gave a soft groan. "Man. Does everyone in your family cook like this?"

"My brother hates to cook."

He opened his eyes. "You've got a brother?"

"He lives in New York."

"City?"

I nodded, sipping my wine.

"Oh, well, he's in the right place then," Tony said. "They've got a billion restaurants, right?"

"I've never been, but I believe there are a lot."

"You haven't been to New York?"

I stirred my salad, picking out a pecan. "No. Joe keeps bugging me to visit."

"Well, you should."

"I will. Someday."

I hadn't seen much of Joe since our father died. He'd come out for the memorial, but he'd only been able to stay overnight.

"What does he do?"

"Joe? He's an investment broker."

"On Wall Street?"

"Yes, I'm afraid so. He claims his company isn't into the high-risk stuff." Privately, I suspected most Wall Street companies were complicit in the bad financial practices that had cost our country so much.

Tony speared another bite of chicken. "Man, this is good."

"Thanks." I smiled, glad to see him eating. After a week of junk food and stress, his body could probably use a more balanced meal.

I ate some chicken, wondering what Tony's customary diet was like. It didn't sound like he cooked much. Did he eat more than one meal a week at his mother's, or did filial stress make it uncomfortable?

"Hey," he said softly.

I looked up. He was smiling.

"You got rid of the hiccups."

"Oh. Yeah."

"Ellen?"

I met his gaze. He put down his knife and fork.

"It's going to get better," he said.

"I hope you're right."

"You've had a rough year."

"I could say the same to you."

He shook his head. "This right now sucks, but I'll get through it. I haven't had to fight the way you have."

"Oh. Well..." My throat tightened unexpectedly. I reached for my wine.

"And I haven't been any help," he added.

"Don't be ridiculous! I'd be a lot worse off if it hadn't been for you."

He took rather a large swallow of wine. "You'd probably be better off if I left you alone."

"What? Where did that come from?"

"I don't want to drag you down."

I stared at him, astonished. This was not the Tony I knew. The one who'd had a chip on his shoulder the size of Manhattan when we met.

"How on earth do you imagine you'd ever drag me down?"

He sighed, gestured to my suite. "You've got all this."

"And a nice, big mortgage, too," I said. "Tony, I work for a living, the same as you. Only you've been at it longer; you've got a strong reputation, a career."

"Yeah. Let's hope I can hang onto that."

"You will. I know you will."

He blinked, then pushed away his wineglass. "I told myself I wouldn't whine."

"You're not."

He rubbed a hand over his face. "I probably should have waited. Come another night. I'm still kind of freaked out."

"I'm glad you didn't wait. We've missed too many chances."

He met my gaze. "Yeah. We have." He reached across the table and took my hand. "Think we'll ever get to that movie?"

I laughed. "I refuse to make a prediction on that one."

He rubbed the ball of his thumb across my knuckle. "It's partly my fault. I get into a case and want to plow through until it's done."

"I can understand that. It must be hard work."

"Well, yeah, but that's not the reason. I love my job. I love what I do. Figuring out problems. Bringing bad guys to justice."

Intensity filled his face, the fire of a hunter on the scent. I'd seen that in him before, but not until now this evening. It gave me a little thrill of hope.

"Angela told me your dad was a policeman," I said.

"Yeah. Beat cop for ten years, then a sergeant. Damn good at it, too."

"And you followed in his footsteps."

"Every time I pick up my badge, put on my gun, I think of him."

Tony's gaze dropped to the table and he swallowed. I recalled the grief I had given him over his gun in the past; I'd asked him not to bring it into the tearoom. I didn't like guns.

It didn't seem to matter so much now.

"Tony, are you wearing your gun?"

"It's evidence. They took it," he said roughly. "They gave me another one to use, but I locked it in my bike. I know you don't like guns."

I squeezed his hand. "Thank you."

This had shaken him. I wasn't surprised, and I wouldn't be surprised if he didn't want to discuss it. What little he'd said was more than I'd expected. Tony was a private person. That he'd allowed me to see even a glimpse of how he felt was, I thought, a great compliment.

"You want some more chicken?"

He looked up from abstraction and shook his head as he let go of my hand. "No, this is great. Gotta save room for dessert, right?" He shot me a smile as he speared a forkful of salad.

"I didn't make a special dessert," I said, "but we can raid the fridge downstairs. There are usually a few sweets left over."

"Abuela really loved those sweets."

"I'm glad."

"She's already talking about coming back."

"She's welcome any time. Will you excuse me for a minute?"

"Sure."

His gaze followed me as I got up and went into my bedroom. I lit two candles there and then returned to the table to finish my meal. I poured more wine for myself and offered more to Tony. He shook his head.

"Better not. Don't want to do anything stupid."

"Why not? I won't tell."

He laughed. "Don't tempt me."

"Shouldn't I?" I ate the last bite of my chicken.

His silence made me look up. He was still watching me.

"I suck at relationships."

"I've heard that said about cops. Doesn't mean it's always true."

"True for me. Ask any of my ex-girlfriends."

"Hm." I took a swallow of wine. "I don't think I can provide any references. My last attempt was in college, and I have no idea where he is by now."

"How long ago?"

"Five years. But who's counting?" I chased down the last bit of pear on my salad plate. "I've been too busy, lately, and before that I was...grieving."

"You make me grateful I still have my mom."

"I've got Nat. Next best thing."

I drained my wineglass, then stood and held out my hand. "I have something to show you."

Tony took my hand and followed me into the bedroom, where I stopped at the foot of the bed. I heard him catch his breath.

"I wondered where you put them," he said. "Thought maybe you got rid of them."

"I wouldn't do that."

Two carved candlesticks, four feet high, flanked my bed, candlelight glowing softly against the walls and the sloping roof, enriching the brocade hangings. They'd been a gift of apology from Tony.

"I tried them all over the house, but this is where they fit best. I've been too shy to tell you."

He turned to me. "Until now?"

I smiled, disengaging my hand from his, but only so I could slide my arms around his waist.

"Until now."

His arms tightened fiercely around me. Hugging him back, I

tried to send him courage, strength, whatever he needed to get through this stressful time. He raised his head, leaning away to stare at me, hurt lingering at the back of his eyes. I laid a hand against his cheek.

"It will get better," I whispered.

The last time Tony had kissed me, it had garnered applause from my staff. If they'd been present for this one, it would have brought down the house.

Nat's Santa Fe Chicken Salad

Ingredients:

1 c cooked chicken, diced
½ c celery, diced
½ c red or yellow bell pepper, diced
½ c jicama, diced
½ c tart apple, diced
1 shallot, minced
¼ c toasted piñon nuts (pine nuts)
¼ c toasted walnuts, chopped
1 T fresh cilantro leaves, chopped
¼ t – ½ t red chile powder
⅛ t celery salt
1 T fresh lime juice
⅓ c mayonnaise

Combine all ingredients in large bowl. Serve on a bed of lettuce, garnish with cilantro leaves, lime wedge, and/or toasted piñon nuts. Serves 3-4.

(Wow, complicated instructions.)

The cilantro and chile powder are optional.

For the apple, I recommend Pink Lady or Cripps Pink, but Granny Smith will do. The pinks are slightly sweeter, but still tart.

Chicken in Brandy Cream Sauce

Ingredients:

1 T butter
1 T olive oil
2 shallots, diced
1 t fresh thyme (or 1/2 t dried)
2 sprigs fresh rosemary (or 2 t
dried)
1/4 c brandy
2-3 T flour
salt to taste
1/2 c cream
2 boneless chicken breasts

Variations:
add 1 c chopped mushrooms
substitute champagne for brandy

Saute shallots in butter and oil. Add rosemary (chopped or crumbled if you wish), thyme, and half the brandy. Add chicken (and mushrooms) and cook gently over low-medium heat (about 20 minutes). Sift in flour, add salt and stir in cream. Stir until sauce thickens (1-4 minutes). Add remaining brandy (or to taste). Serve with rice.

About the Author

Patrice Greenwood was born and raised in New Mexico, and remembers when dusty dogs rolled in the Santa Fe Plaza. She has been writing fiction for over twenty years.

She loves afternoon tea, old buildings, gourmet tailgating at the opera, games, costumes, and solving puzzles. Her popular Wisteria Tearoom Mysteries are informed by many of these interests. She is presently collapsed on her chaise longue, planning the next book in the series.

About Book View Café

Book View Café Publishing Cooperative (BVC) is a an author-owned cooperative of over fifty professional writers, publishing in a variety of genres such as fantasy, romance, mystery, and science fiction.

BVC authors include *New York Times* and *USA Today* bestsellers; Nebula, Hugo, and Philip K. Dick Award winners; World Fantasy and Rita Award nominees; and winners and nominees of many other publishing awards.

In 2008, BVC launched its website, bookviewcafe.com. The cooperative has gained a reputation for producing high-quality ebooks, and is now bringing that same quality to its print editions. Any ebook you purchase from the BVC bookstore returns 95% of the profit directly to the author.

Made in the USA
San Bernardino, CA
16 August 2017